TRAIL OF SECRETS

BOOK THREE

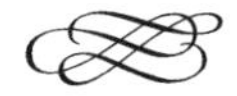

HEIDI VANLANDINGHAM

SHADOWHEART PRESS

Trail of Secrets is a work of fiction. Names, characters, places, and incidents are the product of the author's imagination or are used fictitiously. Any resemblance to actual events, locales, or persons, living or dead, is purely coincidental.

Formerly published under the title *Secrets on the Western Trail*

Contact: Heidi@heidivanlandingham.com

ISBN: 978-1978477568

ALSO BY HEIDI VANLANDINGHAM

IN READING ORDER

For all Buy Links: www.heidivanlandingham.com

Western Trails series

Trail of Hope

Trail of Courage

Trail of Secrets

Mia's Misfits

Mia's Misfits is also in ABC Mail-Order Bride series

Trail of Redemption

American Mail-Order Bride series &

Prequel to Mail-Order Brides of the Southwest

Lucie: Bride of Tennessee

Mail-Order Brides of the Southwest series

The Gambler's Mail-Order Bride

The Bookseller's Mail-Order Bride

The Marshal's Mail-Order Bride

The Woodworker's Mail-Order Bride

The Gunslinger's Mail-Order Bride

The Agent's Mail-Order Bride

WWII

Heart of the Soldier

Flight of the Night Witches

Natalya

Aleksandra

Book 3 available in Fall 2020

Raisa

Of Mystics and Mayhem series

In Mage We Trust

Saved By the Spell

The Curse That Binds

Mistletoe Kisses

Music and Moonlight

Sleighbells and Snowflakes

Angels and Ivy

Nutcrackers and Sugarplums

Box Sets Available

Mail-Order Brides of the Southwest: 3-Book collection

Mistletoe Kisses: 4-book collection

Western Trails: 2-book collection

If you love historical romances, sign up for my reader list, and as a thank you, I'll send you the prequel, a novella, in my Western Trails series.

To download, go to http://tiny.cc/nl-histwest

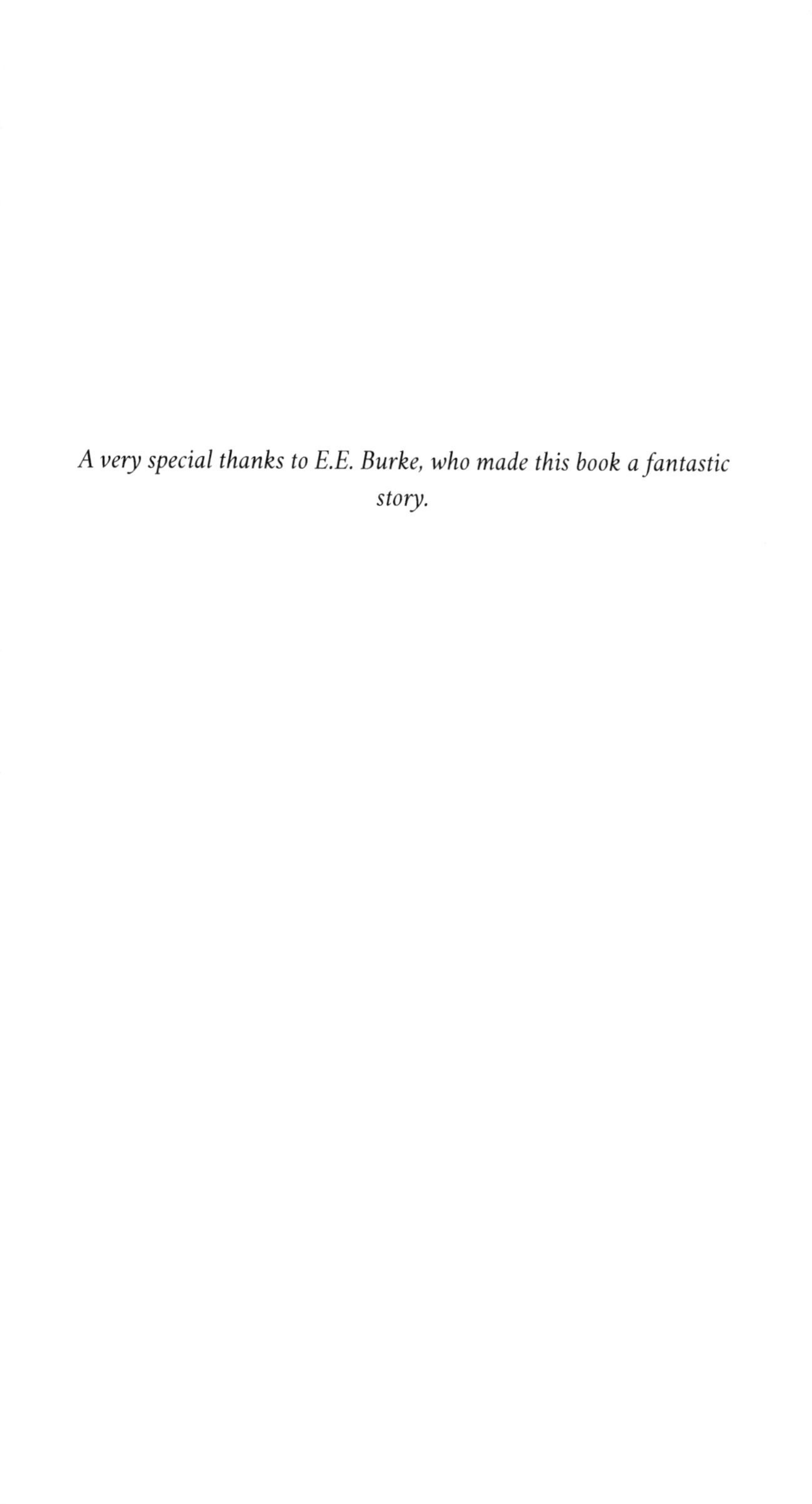

A very special thanks to E.E. Burke, who made this book a fantastic story.

CHAPTER 1

Rancho Sanchez, North Texas, November 1868

A high-pitched whine buzzed by Anna Sanchez's ear. She ducked as a bullet slammed into the stall's support beam behind her. She pulled her pistol from the saddlebag still strapped to her horse and ran to the large door, skidding to a stop when the ranch-hand's body fell backward, landing at her feet. Grabbing his boots, she pulled him inside and turned him over.

She covered her mouth with her gloved hand, staring at his mangled face. Chunks of flesh and shattered teeth were all that was left of his jaw and mouth. She blew out a long breath, and with a trembling hand, closed his sightless eyes. She kicked his feet away from the door and pushed it almost closed, leaving enough space for her to see what was going on outside.

Grabbing for his rifle, she held it to her chest and closed her eyes, pulling in long, slow breaths as she tried to calm her racing heart. She had no idea what was happening, but she'd be damned if she let someone come onto her stepfather's ranch and take everything.

Her eyes popped open as loud war cries rent the air. She peered through the doors, trying to see how many Indians there were, but she couldn't see any. Noise assailed her ears; men screaming in pain, the sound of constant gunfire, and high-pitched cries. Her heart beat out a harsh rhythm against her ribs, and nausea roiled her stomach. She forced a calming breath through her clenched teeth and focused on what she had to do.

A shrill whistle near the barn startled her, pulling her attention from the fight outside to the barely understandable hollering going on at the opposite end of the barn. A rumbling began—low at first, then increasing—until even the ground she kneeled on vibrated from the overwhelming crescendo surrounding her.

She threw a quick glance through the window to where the horses were nervously milling around the fenced corral beside the barn. With terrified gazes, they churned like butter.

Crawling over to the ranch-hand's body, she peered around the edge of the open doorway, only to jerk back from view as a group of riders raced by. The pounding of their hooves was nearly imperceptible amid the roar of the stampeding cattle. She reached down and pulled the pistol from the dead man's hand. After a quick check, she found only one cartridge had been fired. She tucked it behind the waistband of her pants, knowing she'd probably need it.

Taking a deep breath, she counted to three, then eased around the door and into the shadows, holding as still as she could. If someone had stayed behind, she didn't want them to notice her. Glancing around the yard, bodies lay everywhere. Most looked as if they were struck down running for cover;

two hadn't even made it off the porch. And most of the hands had been shot with crude arrows.

She heard the distant thundering as the cattle stampeded through the field. For the first time since the raid had begun, she was able to focus on the attackers instead of dodging bullets. She scowled at the men's retreating figures. There was not a single Indian among them! Fury raced through her like a wildfire. There was only one man strong and stupid enough to attack the Rancho—their neighbor, Wade Phillips.

Only a week ago, she'd tried convincing her stepfather that Phillips was nothing more than a thief and a cur. That the man couldn't be trusted. Instead, he'd believed her mother, who'd convinced him that Anna didn't trust men and was just being silly.

Running back to the barn, she refastened the front saddle cinch, which she'd been undoing when the attack started. She stepped into the stirrup and slid onto the worn leather seat, patting the horse's neck with her gloved hand. Her anger had settled into a fiery determination, and she said a quick prayer that she'd find her stepfather alive and well when she got back.

"Okay, girl," she whispered to her horse. "We've got our job cut out for us. Let's go get us some thieves."

With a tug of the reins and a quick squeeze of her legs, the salt and pepper gray horse trotted from the barn. However, her chase ended before it even began. Facing her in a tight circle were six mounted men—and in the middle, Wade Phillips.

"What are you doing here—you have no right!"

He sat his horse with a smug grin. "Oh, my dear, but I have every right." He pulled something from the inside of his coat and opened it. "You see, Anna, I have the law on my side."

Her eyes widened as she stared at the gently waving paper, dread filling her. "What is that?"

One side of his mouth rose in an evil sneer. "Why, it's the deed to the Rancho. I now own everything on it." One of the men beside him chuckled. "And that includes you."

"I am *not* a thing to be owned. You can go to hell, Phillips!" Hatred burned through her, and she shook like a leaf fluttering in a strong breeze, trying to get a firm grip on her emotions. "Where did you get the deed to my stepfather's Rancho?"

He slowly and meticulously folded the paper, taking his time tucking it back into his pocket and rebuttoning his coat. "Your mama came over to visit me the other day. She gave me what I've been fighting so hard for. The water and you. The cattle are just a bonus."

"You're lying. My mother may not be the most caring person, but she would never do that to me."

"But she did. She knew you would never leave this place and didn't want all her hard work wasted, trying to raise you to act like a lady should. You've been nothing but a disappointment to her, I'm afraid. She left to marry some plantation owner in New Orleans, but wanted to make sure you were at least provided for."

Her breath caught in her throat as she worked to swallow the rising bile. How could her own mother betray her like this? What had she done to deserve such treatment? "You needn't worry," she replied, choking the words out. "My stepfather would never let anything happen to me."

Low laughter filled the silence around her. "I think you will find your stepfather has his own problems—the least of all, you." He walked his horse forward a few steps. "Now, you will come with me."

The self-satisfied grin on his face made her uneasy, and she shook her head. "You will never get me to leave my home!" With a driving urgency to find her stepfather, she kicked her horse harder than she ever had. As the horse charged forward, a loud gunshot sounded, and the horse stumbled. The mare took a few more hesitant steps then stumbled again, dropping to her knees.

As the horse fell on her side, Anna pulled her leg from the stirrup in an attempt to keep from being pinned to the ground. Scrambling to the mare's head, she sobbed, gently rubbing her horse's cheek as the poor animal struggled to breathe. With one last shuddering gasp, the mare died.

Jumping to her feet, Anna whirled around. "You killed her, you—you..." She took one step forward then felt something hard hit the back of her head. Her vision dimmed. She blinked several times and swayed, trying to focus. Her knees buckled and she fell to the ground.

CHAPTER 2

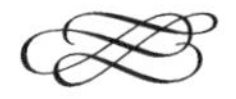

Fort Phantom Hill, Texas

"Mr. Daniels!"

Paul Daniels slung his bedroll behind his saddle and tied it down with piggin' strings. He gave a quick sideways glance to the young soldier jogging down the headquarter building's porch stairs. Without paying him any more mind, he rechecked the cinches, making sure they were secured, giving the dappled gray roan a gentle pat when he was finished.

Glancing at the silvery sky, he knew he was in for some rough weather ahead. Winter was coming early to North Texas, and there were still a lot of miles to travel. He'd promised to be at his sister's in Northwestern Indian Territory for Christmas, and he wasn't about to let her down.

"Mr. Daniels!"

Paul still didn't turn as he grabbed the stirrup and pulled it down into place. He recognized the soldier's clipped Boston accent—kid's name was Potter, if he remembered right. "Name's Paul. And you are?"

"Lieutenant Dean Potter, sir. I have a message for you from the major. A scout rode in about an hour ago, reporting another uprising with the Comanche and Kiowa. Quanah Parker's causing all sorts of ruckus for the troops up north. He wants you to check on the situation for him, seeing how you're going up that way and all."

He stared at the young soldier, noting the grim set of his mouth. His outfit was pristine, which was saying something out here. His hair was trimmed and neat, and the subtle scent of soap still lingered, which told him the kid hadn't been in Texas long. Most men he knew only managed to get a bath once a month.

"Meanin'?" Paul asked.

The kid glanced around behind him and met his gaze. "I don't think it was a request, sir. The major's worried. Rangers, as well as a unit from Camp Wichita, were supposed to come. They should've arrived two days ago, and he doesn't have the men to spare to go looking for them. He said you were a good soldier during the war—best tracker he'd ever seen—and that you'd do the right thing for him now."

Paul swallowed an angry retort. He and Captain Schwan had briefly served together during the latter part of the War Between the States. He'd always figured Schwan would remain in uniform. Some take to a soldier's life. Paul, however, had never wanted to serve in the military. All he wanted was a bit of land where he could run horses, maybe even breed them.

Because of the money, Paul had stayed in for a couple of years after the war's end. But as soon as his term was finished, he'd collected his pay and headed back to Indian Territory. The better part of the last eight years had been spent trying to put memories of battles and death behind him...and even longer searching for the man who'd killed his mother.

Until now, he'd drifted, working as a cowhand or driving cattle up the trails to Kansas. But his nightmares remained. One consolation at least; they seemed to be fading. Instead of every night, they only happened once every week or so. Maybe one day, they would go away completely.

He gave the lieutenant a quick glance. "I wasn't planning on comin' back this way for a while."

Actually, he wasn't planning on ever returning to Texas. He'd delivered the money from his last cattle drive to the owner in San Antonio and had slowly been making his way north to his sister's in the Nation.

From the time he'd been abandoned as a child, he'd been trying to find his mother's killer, but the man seemed to have disappeared. After Christmas, he'd head on to Colorado. If he didn't find anything there, he'd start thinking about his future.

Dean nodded. "Yes, sir. That's why I was ordered to accompany you to Camp Wichita. I'm to send word back with the Rangers, if we can find them, then go further north to Camp Supply where I'm to be stationed."

"How long have you been out here?"

"About a month, sir."

Paul frowned, liking the situation less and less. The last thing he needed was a greenhorn tagging along with him through some of the worst areas of Comancheria. The rest of the Indian Territory seemed tame compared to the area controlled by the Comanche's.

Camp Supply, which was in Kiowa territory, wasn't much better. The last he'd heard, the Kiowa were settling down, at least for the time being. Now that Satanta, one of the sub-chiefs, was back on the reservation, it was anyone's guess as to how long he'd remain.

The camaraderie between the two tribes was also an obstruction the army had to overcome. Where one was, the other wasn't far behind. During the past several years, he'd seen bands of Comanche and Kiowa-Apache joining together for hunting and raids.

"I'm not gettin' rid of you, am I?"

Dean shook his head. "No, sir, you aren't."

Paul sighed, knowing this kid wouldn't find anyone without someone's help. "You have five minutes. If you aren't saddled up and ready, I'm leavin' without you."

The young man took off toward the stables at a run. In less time than he'd been given, he returned, riding a black gelding.

Paul took another deep breath and stepped into the stirrup, throwing one long leg over the saddle. With one arm draped over the horn, he glanced back at the lieutenant. "I'll say this one time and one time only. You do as I say, when I say. Got that?"

Dean's eyes widened. "Of course, sir."

He bit back a chuckle. "West Point?"

The young man frowned. "Yes, sir. How did you know, sir?"

"Easy on the 'sirs'. Name's Paul. And I knew the moment you started talkin', kid."

Leading them away from the small fort, his thoughts turned inward. Underneath his jokes and smiles lurked a simmering rage. He'd only been five years old when his life had fallen apart, and the man who'd caused it all—he'd never forget that bastard's face.

There were only a few good memories from his childhood—his mother's long, black, silky hair, her wide smile. Her safe hugs. He had no memories of his father, only his mother's sadness. Even more vivid was the memory of the man who had taken them in, given them shelter. The dark visage of the man who'd beaten his mother to death and left him for dead somewhere on the Kansas prairie.

One day he'd find that man and kill him…but until then, he would keep wandering. Keep searching.

SEVERAL MILES south of Red River Station, Paul and Dean topped a low hill overlooking the yard of a large, Mexican-style house. The beauty of the house faded into the background when Paul noticed the bodies.

One lay over the porch rail and another face down on the stairs. There were more scattered around the large yard, most with one or two arrows protruding from their backs. As they got closer, he saw more men just inside the corral… two of the four had arrows in them as well.

As they walked their horses into the yard, Paul's gaze moved along the ground, picking out the shod prints of twelve horses, at least…but no unshod hooves, which the Indians would've been riding. Due to the chewed up ground, it was impossible for him to tell exactly how many had plowed through here.

He climbed down and stretched, his muscles tight from the long hours in the saddle. Winding the reins around the top runner of the small fenced-in corral, he glanced over the bodies, worry nagging at him.

He walked over to the nearest body and squatted, resting his weight on the heels of his boots. The man had been young—twenty-something—and was just beginning to fill out in the shoulders. His shirt and pants were torn, as if he'd been dragged.

Paul counted three bullet holes, two in his chest. The third had taken out a chunk of skin from his neck. Leaning forward, he gently closed the dead man's eyes, sorrow for such needless deaths filling his heart.

"Sir? Can you tell which tribe attacked these people? I'll need to send a report back to Major Schwan. We also need to check the house and barn for survivors."

Paul pointed toward the well. "Water the horses and check everyone in the yard and the corral. Make sure they're all dead. I'll look inside the buildings."

He glanced toward the house, a quick frown shadowing his eyes, dreading what he might find inside. The heavy planked front door stood ajar, the interior dark. He held himself still and listened to the complete silence around him.

The only sound he heard came from the chomping of their horses behind him as they snapped at the tufts of brown grass growing from beneath the fence. Even with the shortage of fall rain over the past couple of years, the grass remained tenacious as it forged new roots into the surrounding sandy soil.

"Think Comanches did this?"

Paul ignored the kid's question and continued to stare at the house, a bad feeling churning in his gut. The bodies had already stiffened, so he knew whoever attacked the Rancho was long gone, but that didn't mean they wouldn't be back. "Sit tight, Potter. I'll be right back."

He entered the barn, his eyes quickly adjusting to the dim light. The structure was larger than most he'd seen, other than military stables. He counted twelve stalls on either wall, the stall ropes hanging to the floor.

Two stalls in, he found another body. With the toe of his boot, he flipped him over. The man had been shot in the neck and shoulder. Further in, he found two more bodies and wondered if they were the defenders or the attackers.

His boots clopped against the wood planks, loud in the heavy silence, as he made his way to the closed door at the back of the barn. It wasn't unusual for Indians to use guns; most of the tribes had them, either by trading or killing for them. However, this attack didn't feel like Indians to him. He couldn't put his finger on it yet...but he would.

He pushed the door open, expecting to see the corrals. Instead, he found himself in a smithy. The central fire pit, normally hot enough to melt metal, was cold. He picked up the large tongs and turned them over, their heavy weight unfamiliar in his grip.

From the size and well-kept condition of the structures, the workers hadn't been gone long, but in this harsh landscape, it wouldn't take much time for nature to begin reclaiming the land.

He'd been through this area enough to know that no amount of money kept anyone safe out here. From talking to the soldiers at the fort, this part of Texas was under the constant threat of raids by both the Comanche and Kiowa-Apache. The Indians had never bothered him when he'd traveled through, but he still kept a wary gaze, never letting his guard down...and he wasn't about to start now.

Leaving the barn, he made his way along the sandy path running toward the house. Several times he stopped and examined the bodies as well as the surrounding ground, then walked up to the front porch. He pulled the man down from the railing, laying him on his back, then pulled out the arrow protruding from his right shoulder. The arrow hadn't killed him, but the knife wound to the heart did. From what he could tell, none of the men died from an arrow wound.

"Dean! Keep an eye open. The men who attacked this ranch weren't Indians."

The lieutenant's dark gaze skimmed over the yard. "White men? You're sure?"

Paul held out the arrow and tossed it to the ground in front of him. "No Indian would ever use an arrow like that. Looks like a child made it. And none of the arrows were kill shots."

He turned and pushed the door, which lightly thudded against the small dividing wall separating the expansive living area from the smaller dining room. Inside, the interior was reminiscent of a Mexican hacienda, the openness allowing the chilly fall breeze to flow through the rooms. He glanced at the sheer red curtains fluttering away from the open windows.

Overhead, a long, rough-hewn dark brown beam ran the length of the high ceiling and several smaller beams jutted out like ribs on either side. The room was filled with large, comfortable-looking leather furniture, worn and faded at the outer edges. His eyes were drawn to a massive bookcase spanning the entire wall, the shelves empty.

He frowned. Papers still covered the heavy desk, some strewn across the clay-tiled floor, but the bookshelves were empty. A couple of vases, still filled with bouquets of wilted flowers, rested on the two round tables sitting at each end of the sofa. On one, several gold coins lay scattered across the top. If this had been a robbery, they wouldn't have left the coins behind...unless they'd only been after the cattle.

He clenched his jaw, his gaze drawn to where the inner corner of the curtain gently waved above a small table. Fear welled up inside of him, his nerves as taut as a bowstring. He stared at a small daguerreotype of a dark-haired girl, her beautiful face shining out from the silver halo.

He breathed a quick prayer for the girl's safety before moving slowly through the wide doorway of the colorful kitchen, then coughed as the smell of death filled his nostrils. Bright yellow and green Mexican tiles covered the walls, giving the room a cheerful façade...but it was just that. A façade.

Walking toward the open back door, he stopped short when he saw the decomposing body of a plump, gray-haired woman lying face-down on the red tile floor. She'd been shot through the chest; the dark brown blood had spread out in a large pool beneath her.

He closed his eyes, sorrow choking him like a garrote. He forced his heavy feet to walk down the narrow hall to stand in front of a hand-hewn oak door. He hesitated, dread filling his body. He closed his eyes and wrapped his hand around the doorknob. He didn't want to find the girl's lifeless body behind the closed door. He'd seen too many dead bodies during the war. Everywhere he went, the specter of death seemed to follow.

Silence hung heavy over the house, and the small hairs on the back of his neck stood on end. He forced his eyes open and turned the cool metal knob, slowly pushing the door open.

Inside was a massive, shiny brass bed. Glass from the window showered across the floor. Crunching with each step, he walked toward the open window but stopped when he rounded the bed.

On the floor was the body of a well-dressed man. Tall and thin, he, too, lay in a pool of blood. The fury of the attack was evident from the jagged wound almost severing his head.

Paul's heels clunked loudly in the silence house as he hurried outside. Indians hadn't caused these deaths, but he was going to find out who had. This wasn't something he could just walk away from—not until he found the little girl. Stepping into the saddle, he glanced at Dean, already sitting astride his horse.

"Did you find anyone alive?"

Paul shook his head. "Two dead inside. What do you make of this?"

Before Dean could answer, he heard the pounding of hooves and stepped his horse around as a small group of tired-looking riders rode into the yard.

The dust-covered men surrounded them in a loose semicircle facing them, effectively pinning them in place. The leader, evident from the uniform stripes on his dusty military jacket, touched two outstretched fingers against the bill of his hat in a quick greeting then dropped his hand to rest against his thigh.

"Evenin' gentlemen. Major Josiah Carpenter." He nodded with a jerk of his head to his men. "These are my men. Part of a larger group of Texas police chasing after the Comanche. The Quahadis raided several nearby farms. Made off with about twenty horses and five to six hundred cattle."

"State police?" Paul asked.

"Since Governor Davis took the reins, we're police, but we prefer to be called Rangers. Came by here to check on everyone here. Guess they didn't fare so well."

The major twisted in the saddle and glanced around the yard then faced them again. "Too many dead men here for neither of you to have a scratch. Find 'em like this?"

Paul nodded. "Yes, sir. We're headin' to Red River Station then on to Camp Wichita."

The major backed his horse up and turned toward the dead men, his gaze focused on the ground around them. "Comanches?" He squinted at one of the bodies, moving his horse closer. "Hmm. Somebody tried real hard to make us believe this here was done by Indians."

"Yes sir, they did. Noticed there weren't any unshod tracks anywhere around the yard—and the arrows are wrong," Paul said as he rode up beside him. "Did you know the people living here?"

Carpenter nodded. "Known Jonathan Sanchez for about a year now. Nice enough fellow, but a bit strange. Always wearin' a suit. His wife is another story. Most beautiful lady I've ever seen, but ice runs through her veins. Cold-hearted. Never could see what he saw in her."

"Did they have a young daughter?"

With his head tipped forward slightly, the brim of his hat keeping most of the sun's bright glare out of his eyes, he chewed on the end of his unlit cigarette. "Only daughter I ever saw was..." He scrunched his face in thought. "Now what was her name? Anna. Her name was Anna, but she's in her twenties. Did you find her inside? Right shame. Sweet girl and just as pretty as her mother."

"No sir. There was an older Mexican woman and from the way he was dressed, I'd say the gentleman in the bedroom was Sanchez."

Carpenter's thoughtful gaze swept over the yard. "Think anyone else made it? Sanchez usually kept ten or so hands out with the cattle when he was gatherin' them up for a fall roundup."

Paul felt drawn and tired, but knew he couldn't let the girl fend for herself against someone who could orchestrate something as heinous as this was. For some reason, the little girl's pretty face on the daguerrotype, her smile filled with the hope and innocence of youth, had touched his heart. He couldn't help but to offer his assistance. "As I said earlier, we were headin' north. But we have time enough for a search party, if you'd like the extra help."

Dean nodded in agreement. "Damn straight we're helping." He threw a sideways glance to the major. "Sir."

"Hell, son," the major said to Paul. "We need all the help we can get out here." He motioned with a wide swing of his arm overhead, and, without a word, his men rode through the open corral gait and spread out.

Paul nodded to Dean. "Let's head to the river and search there." Riding through the field at an easy gallop, he kept a wary gaze on the skeletal trees running along the horizon. Pulling up the collar of his black overcoat to keep the chilly wind off his neck, he led Dean into the trees, which followed a rough outline of the Rancho's northern border.

Nothing stood out until he made his way through a particularly thick tangle of bushes growing over the path when he caught sight of something fluttering. Slowing his horse, he leaned sideways and scooped up a torn piece of calico print stuck to the broken limb of a dead bush.

He turned it over a couple of times, his thumb rubbing the soft fabric. It looked like material from a woman's blouse. Although, the small fragment could've been out here for weeks and been from anyone's shirt. He tucked the scrap into his coat pocket.

A shrill whistle pierced the air, east of where they were, but Paul continued along the narrow trail, Dean following behind him. Tall grasses and weeds had long covered the path, which disappeared when they left the trees.

Running into the wind, the cold burned Paul's face, and his eyes watered. They rounded a small plateau, lines of tan soil layered between a wide expanse of red dirt above and below. Beside the narrow river were the Rangers. Two of the riders knelt a few feet away, looking at someone lying on the ground.

Dismounting, Paul moved to stand just behind the two kneeling men. Rising, they shook their heads at Major Carpenter and moved away. He glanced at the broken body of the injured man. His eyes opened and stared up at him. He tried to say something and coughed, pink foam on his lips.

He dropped to one knee and leaned closer. The man's black hair was matted with blood and sand. There was a wicked gash along one cheek, and his limbs were mangled and twisted. "What's your name, cowboy?"

He coughed up more blood, choked a bit, and then cleared his throat as he met Paul's gaze. "Robert James. Find her. My fault...the cattle...*cough, cough*...stampeded."

"Find who?"

"Anna Sanchez." He choked. "Paid us…to move cattle… north." The dying man's voice faded.

Paul leaned forward. "RJ, whose plans?"

"Her mother's and Phillips'—didn't know he was goin' to take her..." He closed his eyes and he struggled for breath. His eyes popped open and he grabbed Paul's arm. "On way to ranch to warn her… Cattle spooked."

He took another shallow breath, his chest shuddering under the strain, then he let out a long sigh. Eyes wide open, his head slowly dipped to the ground.

With a surge of frustration and worry for the missing girl, Paul rose and faced the major. "Who is this man, Phillips?"

"A no-account scoundrel and thief. Like a rattlesnake, he'd rather kill a person than work. Lazy, but ruthless."

While chewing thoughtfully on the inside of his cheek, the major rolled a cigarette. Taking a long draw, he blew out the blue-white smoke from his nostrils. "We'll go after him together. Had a few run-ins with him. Might be more willing to cooperate if he sees me." He glanced at two wiry men who looked like they hadn't eaten in a month. "Smith, Corbin, follow the cattle. We'll catch up as soon as we find Miss Sanchez."

The two men raised their arms and momentarily rested their hands against the brims of their hats. Like partners in a dance, they turned their horses in unison and raced across the river.

Dean stepped forward and saluted Carpenter. "Permission to speak, sir."

The major nodded.

"I have orders to find information about a Ranger outfit sent to find a couple of soldiers due in from Camp Wichita two days ago. Would you, by chance, be those Rangers?"

"No, Lieutenant. Passed a group up near there headin'

north toward Camp Supply late yesterday. Maybe they're the ones you're lookin' for?"

Dean gave a quick nod, his lips pinched together in frustration.

Carpenter took one last drag on his cigarette then crushed it against the seam of his trousers and dropped it to the ground. He loosely held his reins in the palm of one hand. "Let's go pay a visit to Mr. Wade Phillips, boys."

CHAPTER 3

Anna Sanchez was furious with herself for letting her guard down. How could she have been so stupid? Her brain worked at a furious pace to figure out a way to escape from the small room. The only result was a massive headache.

For the hundredth time, she pushed against the window, trying to force it to open. And like the other ninety-nine times, it didn't budge. Earlier, she'd broken the glass, also managing to slice her finger on a small nail protruding from the thin wooden muntins that divided the window into sections.

She was still trapped because of the thinly spaced metal bars on the window's exterior. They had been securely anchored to the house and prevented her from pushing them away from the house so that she could crawl through the window. Apparently, Wade Phillips had thought of everything.

With disgust, she sat on the edge of the bed, her heart aching over her mother's betrayal. She's grown up with the woman's machinations—money and prestige were the only things she cared about. Mama had told her as much not two weeks ago during one of her daily rants about how she wished to return to her home in New Orleans, and how horrible her husband treated her.

The ranch hands lying dead back home had been her friends. Her family. If only her stepfather had listened when she'd tried to tell him how horrible Wade Phillips was, none of them would be dead. Memories swamped her: the older men watching out for her, keeping her out of trouble, the younger hands taking a few precious minutes out of their day to teach her how to rope and ride. For them and her stepfather, she vowed to kill Wade Phillips for what he'd done.

The only thing her mother had ever given her was grief. The woman would never understand her. Anna didn't care about dresses and balls or fancy French pastries. From the moment she'd set foot on her stepfather's land, she'd known what she wanted to do with her life. She wanted to run the Rancho. And she wanted to marry for love, not money as her mother always had.

She shivered at the memory of her mother's cold blue gaze as she'd said there was no such thing as love. She'd known something was up when her mother had started complaining about her only daughter being a spinster...even threatening her with marriage, no matter who the man. Well, now she knew. "You won't get away with this, Mama. I won't marry him," she muttered to the empty room.

Staring through the window without really seeing anything, Anna realized her options weren't good. Before leaving, her mother had, indeed, followed through with her threat. She had given her to the worst man possible.

The first time she'd met him he'd reminded her of a

snake. The second time, she'd changed her opinion, deciding he was more like a toad, warts and all.

Walking back to stand by the window, she raised her face to the heavy breeze moving through the room, clearing the slimy feeling from her mind. Without the glass, she didn't feel so confined, and every once in a while she could hear the men talking on the front porch which was how she'd learned her stepfather was dead.

She'd heard a man laugh and tell someone they were moving Jonathan Sanchez's cattle north to Camp Wichita to be sold to the army since Red River Station was too close to risk selling stolen cattle. Her stepfather would never let anyone take, much less sell, his cattle. Not without a fight. If the cattle were gone, the ranch was nothing. If she had any hope of running the ranch, she'd have to get the cattle back.

She fought back the tears for such a senseless death. Jonathan Sanchez had given her a father's love at a time when she'd needed it the most. The person she'd grown up to be— hardworking, honest, caring, and loyal—was all because of him.

Two men stood in the doorway of the large barn at the far end of the yard. The larger one held a rifle, cradling it like a baby, his face black and blue from a beating. The other man's rifle lay propped against the door while he whittled. She stared at the knife as it cut the small piece of wood.

Listening to the quiet interior of the house, she was greeted by silence. No sounds, no voices. Unless the guard on the other side of her door had disappeared too, which she doubted, the window was her only hope of escape. However slim a chance that was, she'd have to keep trying to loosen the metal bars. Wade Phillips was anything but stupid. He would never leave her unguarded, inside the house or out.

The dark cherry wood furniture in the small room seemed out of place in these rugged lands. The chairs' and dressing tables' legs resembled matchsticks compared to the rugged design of her stepfather's. One giant man sneeze and the thin-spindled legs would snap in two. Her eyes narrowed thoughtfully as she stared at the chair with the beginning of an idea.

How hard would it be to break one off? She turned it over to find that they were secured to the seat with rough, square-headed screws. She'd have to break the leg off. Wrapping her hand around the bottom spindle of the thin leg, she pushed and pulled, trying to work it loose. The furniture wasn't as fragile as she'd thought. The thing wouldn't budge.

Frustrated, she stood up and kicked the leg several times. Finally, with a loud *cra-ack* she fell forward against the chair, stopping her fall by grabbing the edge of the seat.

Suddenly, a gunshot echoed from outside, followed by men's shouts. More gunshots followed. The guard yelled, and the vibrating slam of the front door told her he'd run outside.

As she glanced through the window bars, she wondered who was shooting at whom, a small hope blossomed in the back of her mind that someone had actually come to rescue her. If they hadn't, then they could kill each other off. All she wanted to do was escape.

Several riders charged by her window. Two of them veered off and rode toward the barn. The two men she'd seen earlier were now lying on the ground, not moving. She hoped they were dead. The older one had been her first guard, until Phillips caught him trying to kiss her. He'd been beaten so badly, the purple bruises were just beginning to fade.

She tugged against the bars, willing them to break off. She managed to loosen them but not enough. At this rate, she'd never escape.

Holding the bars, she watched the second rider, a newcomer, fall to the ground then roll, hiding by the barn wall. The other man had already disappeared, his silver-grey horse standing in the open doorway. The hazy form of a man appeared from behind the horse, and her breath caught in her throat. She held it a moment, letting it out between the narrow space between her lips when he moved out of the shadows.

Brown hair curled over his collar, but his face remained hidden underneath his black hat. He was slender, moving like a cat. His movements were fluid and sure. Even slouched over like he was, she knew when he stood upright, he would be tall. She couldn't tell, but his boots looked worn, and there seemed to be splotches on his black trousers. Dirt, maybe? Underneath his dark black coat, she caught a glimpse of a gray shirt.

Her gaze was drawn to the empty gun holster against his thigh. She pressed her face closer against the window, trying to see if there was another one against his other leg. He turned toward the edge of the barn and said something. He was either talking to the man on the other side of the wall or himself. He shifted his position, and she caught a quick glimpse of his other leg. No second gun. She breathed a soft sigh of relief. So he wasn't a gunslinger then. *Who were these men?*

In a well-practiced motion, he shoved his hat back on the crown of his head. She blinked, her eyebrows rising. She blinked again. "Please be here to rescue me," she whispered.

Suddenly, the man lunged behind the barn door and with quick movements, fired his pistol several times. Both horses jumped out of the way and the young man hiding by the building scurried around the corner and into the barn. He was dressed in military blues.

Who were they? At least one was a soldier, so hopefully the others with him were too…

Another volley of gunfire sounded, this time answered by

several high-pitched screams. A loud whine whistled by her head, followed by a muted *thwup.* Jerking away from the window, she dropped to a crouch, her breath coming in quick gasps. On the other side of the room was a hole in the wall where a bullet had struck.

Inching toward the glass, she looked out but kept her face as close to the sill as she could in case another bullet came her way. She growled in frustration. How in the hell was she supposed to get out of here?

Men hollered back and forth, but none of the voices were familiar to her. A silent scream of aggravation stuck in her throat as she ran back to the door and pounded against the hard wood with the sides of her fists. She jerked on the door-knob as hard as she could, a frantic surge of desperation adding to her strength, but the door wouldn't budge. She kicked it with her boot and grumbled as a sharp pain shot up through her toes.

On the other side of the door the foreman's voice was muted, but grew louder along with his booted footsteps. Close to the door, he yelled at one of the men to grab his horse and take it out back, Before she could pull her hand away from the knob, the door opened, shoving hard against her.

She stumbled backward, trying to catch her balance. Her gaze landed on the broken chair leg lying at her feet. She reached down and grabbed it, only to have the foreman wrap his arms around her and pull her up against him.

She threw her head back against his head. He dropped his arms. Jerking around, she saw him clasping his bloody nose with his hands as he cursed. She picked up the leg and hit him across the side of his head as hard as she could.

She scrambled around him as he moaned on the floor, and raced down the hallway, through the large living room, and toward the screen door. Hearing him coming up behind her, she lunged for the door but wasn't quick enough. The foreman's hand grabbed her around the neck and jerked her backward as he pushed open the door with his other hand, shoving her onto the back porch.

Falling forward, she dropped the chair leg as she stumbled off the porch and landed in a heap in the dirt.

He swiped the blood off his face with his sleeve. "I can see why Mr. Phillips has such a keen interest in you, hellcat. Got orders to get you away from here, and that's what I aim to do —even if it kills me."

She glanced at her only weapon lying at his feet on the porch. "If you touch me again, I *will* kill you."

He laughed and reached to pick up the piece of wood, slapping it against his palm as he walked down the stairs toward her. He jerked her to her feet and hauled her none-too-gently toward a saddled horse, the reins dangling on the ground as he chewed on several dead plants at the base of a thin oak tree near the corner of the back porch.

He hefted her over the pommel like a sack of flour, wedging her hipbone against the hard leather of the saddle horn. Kicking her legs out, she twisted her body, trying to push herself off the horse. Each movement only wedged her tighter as he tied her in place.

Loud reports of gunshots echoed through the air, but she was on the wrong side of the house. The fighting was taking place in front. She was in the back and on her own. Pulling as much air as she could into her constricted lungs, she let out a frustrated scream, praying someone would hear her.

The foreman's large hand slapped over her mouth, and she promptly bit the tender webbing between his finger and thumb. He let out a curse and with the back of his hand, smacked her across the cheek. He raised the other hand, the broken chair leg gripped in his fist.

"I wouldn't touch the lady again if I were you," a low voice drawled.

She craned her head around to see who it was but only saw the horse, its floppy lips nibbling at what was left of the leaves on a nearby branch. She shivered in the cold air, wishing she had a coat, but knew not having one was the least of her worries.

"Back off, mister. This here is none of your business," the foreman said.

"Well, guess I'm making it my business. Seems to me you have two choices: let the lady down easy like, or draw."

The foreman scoffed. "You're bluffing. You wouldn't risk hitting her."

"Try me."

Anna's blood chilled at the icy tone in the stranger's voice, and she lay still. Did she want to be rescued by this man? He could be worse than Phillips…

"Your gun's already drawn. That doesn't give me much of a chance, now does it?" the foreman asked.

Something slid against leather, and she struggled to raise her head higher, craning her neck like a turtle to see what was happening.

"There. Now we're evenly matched." The stranger's flat voice sent chills over her body.

The foreman jerked his gun from behind his waistband. Before he cleared leather, she heard the whine of a bullet and a harsh grunt. She felt his body jerk behind her, and his gun fired, but the shot struck the dirt near the base of the tree. She held her breath as he slid off the horse, dropping to the ground with a *thud*.

She stared into his wide-open eyes, a surprised expression on his face. The rope loosened and fell between the horse's hooves. A pair of hands grabbed her around the waist and pulled her from the horse.

"Excuse me, ma'am, but are you all right?"

She nodded without looking at him. Her hand crept upward and clasped the base of her throat. She could feel her heart racing underneath the pads of her fingers, and she couldn't seem to stop the shivers wrenching her body.

When she finally raised her head, Anna was unable to pull her gaze away from the handsome cowboy she'd seen through the bedroom window. His face was hawkish, with an aquiline nose and prominent cheekbones. His jacket hung open, showing narrow hips and a flat stomach. Pale green eyes stared back at her. Suddenly feeling frumpy, she reached up and tried to re-tuck her hair into her coiled braid. Drowning in his gaze, she cleared her throat and forced the words from her dry mouth. "I am...I'm Anna Sanchez. And you are?"

"Name's Paul Daniels. The major will be relieved you're safe. If you'll follow me, I'll take you to him."

"The major? I don't know any major. Just like I don't know you. What makes you think I'm stupid enough to follow you anywhere?"

He shrugged, his hard gaze holding no emotion as he stared at her. "Suit yourself." Turning, he walked away.

She quickly picked up the table leg and scurried after the long-legged man as he strode around to the front of the house. She turned the corner behind him and jerked to a stop, almost running into his backside as he climbed onto the back of his horse.

"Miss Sanchez?"

She glanced toward the gruff voice and met the grey eyes of an older man. Sun and wind had leathered his skin, making it hard to judge his age. His long black mustache rose as he smiled at her, a cigarette hanging between yellowed teeth.

She sighed. "Yes?"

His smile widened. "Major Josiah Carpenter of the Texas State Police."

Anna pinched the top of her nose as she tried to thwart her growing headache. "Thank you for rescuing me, major. Did you catch him?"

"Sorry, ma'am. Haven't found Phillips yet. I have my men searchin' as we speak. If it hadn't been for your foreman we wouldn't have known where to look."

"I take it then you were at the Rancho—did you find my stepfather?" She bit back a sob, her grip tightening around the chair leg still in her hand. "And our hands? Did you find anyone alive?"

"Do you plan on using that?" The young soldier she'd seen earlier pointed to her side.

She frowned at him then slowly shook her head, realizing how useless her little weapon was against guns, and let it slide to the ground. Not that she thought they would hurt her, but after everything she'd been through in the last few days, she wasn't sure who to trust anymore.

"Did you think to give him a splinter?"

Mr. Daniels's voice was no longer sharp, and she could now hear a pleasant western drawl. His words, however, annoyed her. She pinched her lips together and counted only to five. Ten was too long. "Would you like to find out? Even a splinter can fester." She gave him a sickly sweet smile, ignoring the young soldier's chuckle.

Still staring at him, she couldn't be sure, but thought she saw the hint of a twinkle in his green eyes.

She turned back to the major and wrapped her shaking arms around her middle, blinking back the tears rapidly filling her eyes as her adrenaline wore off. She took a deep breath and let her anger take over. There would be plenty of time to mourn after Phillips was caught and made to pay for her stepfather's death.

She forced out the held breath as her lungs screamed for air. For the first time since all of this had happened, she realized that with her stepfather gone, she had no home. Nowhere to go. She refused to follow her mother to New Orleans, which was probably exactly what she was expecting Anna to do. In that moment, she made up her mind. She was going to fight for the Rancho—buy it back if necessary. But in order to do that, she had to have the missing cattle.

"Major, do you know where they took the cattle?"

His brows dipped together in a frown. "Your foreman told us they'd already headed them north. I know what you're thinkin' ma'am. Let 'em go. You can't drive them by yourself. With your ranch hands injured or dead, it can't be done."

She scowled. "I refuse to give up that easily, major. Will you please take me back to the ranch? My foreman can help me. We will gather up some men—"

"Miss Sanchez, I hate to be the one to tell you, but…I'm sorry, ma'am, but your foreman's dead," Paul said.

Her lower lip trembled, and she held a hand to her queasy stomach. "Oh, RJ...he was my friend."

"He also told us Phillips paid the men to take the cattle north. He wanted you to know he had no knowledge of the plan to kidnap you," the major added.

With a couple of quick blinks, her teary gaze disappeared and a fist tightened around her heart. How many more people were going to betray her?

"I need to get back to the ranch for supplies. I'm going after the cattle. My stepfather worked too hard for what he had. I can't just sit back and let Phillips steal everything!"

The major's gray eyes squinted. "Miss Sanchez, I'm afraid I can't let you do that. You don't stand a chance out there alone, and I don't have the men to spare to help you. You need to come with us to Red River Station where you will be safe until we find Phillips."

She shook her head, too many emotions swirling around inside of her. Why did these men not understand? Her stepfather had been so good to her—a loving father. He'd filled the void left after her brother, Richard, died. She was going to fight for the ranch as Jonathan Sanchez would have done, because it was all she had left.

Carpenter cleared his throat. "This area isn't safe for anyone, more so for a woman like you. Comanches would love nothing more than finding a lone female in their midst. The Quahadis are raiding, and we've been ordered to find and stop them. You will be dropped off at Camp Wichita." He turned and motioned with a pointed finger at one of his Rangers. "Jones, go saddle up a horse for Miss Sanchez."

With her fists clenched at her sides, she glared at him. "My stepfather always talked about making a drive—running a herd west of the Chisholm Trail. They thought the terrain was easier to travel and the cattle wouldn't lose as much weight. One of the times Captain John Lytle stayed at the ranch, Phillips joined us for dinner. The men talked all night, planning a route across the western part of the Nation. If they're heading anywhere, they're heading up the route they discussed that night."

She knew she was right about this, and somehow, she was going to have to convince Major Carpenter to let her go to Camp Wichita. She took a step forward. "He was my father. He taught me how to ride my first horse and rope my first calf. He was proud of what he'd built and instilled in me that same pride. The ranch is his legacy. I owe it to him to finish this. The ranch is lost without that herd." She placed a trembling hand on the hand resting against his thigh. "Please help me..."

The major scowled at her. "That's suicide, miss. Land

there is filled with Kiowa-Apache and Comanche. It's their hunting grounds. Not even the army travels through those lands. Desolate prairie, flat and near waterless. No place to hole up and hide if attacked. A person can get lost—no landmarks to go by. You'll be easy target practice for anyone who comes across your trail."

She crossed her arms over her chest and met his hard gaze with one of her own. "It's a risk I'm willing to take."

Major Carpenter chewed on his cigar, switching it from one side to the other in a frustrated scowl. Finally, he glanced at Paul. "Son, you're goin' to Camp Wichita."

"Yes, but—"

Carpenter shook his head. "No buts. Either you take her or she has to come with us. My orders are to scout the area for the renegade Comanches stealing from the ranches around here. I don't have the time to take her. I also can't spare any of my men."

Paul leaned against the pommel and stared at the back of his horse's head, watching the subtle twitching of his black ears. The last thing he wanted was to take her with them, but he knew that tone. The major hadn't been asking. His hard gaze and flat tone had been stating.

Anna moved to stand beside his horse. "Please, Mr. Daniels…"

He glanced down at her slim throat, watching as she swallowed. Dark smudges on the sides of her neck were already turning black and blue. If he hadn't already killed the foreman, he would have enjoyed beating him to death for hurting her. No man should lay a hand on a woman.

A woman's face, battered and swollen, flashed through his mind, but he quickly shoved it back to wherever it had come from. Some things, in his opinion, were better left buried.

He pulled his gaze back up to her pretty face. Something about this woman tugged at him. She was stubborn and put up a good front, but he could see the pain in her eyes. He understood the pain of being alone in the world, not knowing who to turn to or where to go. He couldn't believe he was even entertaining the notion of helping her, but he knew he wouldn't be able to live with himself if he didn't.

Growing up, his adopted family had always joked about how soft-hearted he was. Getting his sister, Megan, out of trouble had been his self-appointed job. There wasn't a single thing he wouldn't do for his family.

"Please," she whispered again.

He met her dark brown gaze for a moment, then with a small sigh, turned his attention back to the major. "If Miss Sanchez is hell bent on getting her cattle back, then we can take her as far as Camp Wichita. There might be a good chance of getting help there."

Anna gave Paul a tremulous smile. "Thank you, Mr. Daniels."

"It's too late to head out. We'll go back to your ranch tonight and pack up what we'll need, getting an early start in the morning." He glanced up at the dark gray clouds filling the sky. "If the weather holds, we'll make Camp Wichita in two and a half days, maybe three.

"Miss Sanchez, I was raised by a good family who taught me to take care of and respect womenfolk. You're safe with me." With a quick tilt of his head and shrug of his shoulder toward the young man by his side, he added, "I can vouch for Dean too."

ANNA STARED into Paul's light green eyes. For some unknown reason, his gaze calmed the rapid beating of her pulse, and her jittery stomach relaxed.

"Okay," she sighed, hoping she didn't come to regret her hasty decision. "I'll go with you back to the Rancho.

Major Carpenter gave them a quick nod and motioned for the Rangers to move out with a flip of his thick wrist. "Miss Sanchez, I think you're crazy, but I wish you luck." He met Paul's gaze. "I'm trusting you to take care of her. Don't make me come after you too. Now, we're off to find a particularly ornery bunch of Comanches."

CHAPTER 4

Anna hunched down into her coat but still wasn't close to being warm. The skin on her face was so cold she couldn't feel it anymore. The frigid air from the harsh winter storm front had seeped into her bones. One strong bump and they'd shatter.

Clamping her jaws together to keep her teeth from chattering, she stared at the barren landscape. Surrounding them was a panorama of rolling plains; the tall, red-tinged golden grasses seemed never ending.

She couldn't help but wonder if these men knew what they were doing, or even where they were taking her. If Indians showed up now, the three of them would be dead. There was no place to hide.

She stared at Paul's back as he rode tall in the saddle, his wide-brimmed, flat-crowned black hat pulled low over his face to ward off the falling snow. Dressed all in black, his gun tied to his right thigh, he reminded her of a gunslinger... although from what RJ had told her, most of them nowadays wore two strapped-down guns.

She'd learned at a young age to judge a man by his actions. Daniels seemed to be quiet, not one movement wasted. The way his gaze never stopped moving told her he didn't miss much.

A low rumble shook her stomach, ending in another long growl. "Umm, Mr. Daniels, are we going to be able to stop soon? Lunchtime was two hours ago. Can we please stop soon and eat—I'm starving."

"Name's Paul. Don't know a Mr. Daniels."

She stared at him a moment then smiled, her chapped lips cracking, from the constant onslaught of the north winds. "You're strange."

"Is that a compliment or an insult?"

"I'm not sure yet. Shouldn't we have come across the herd by now?"

"We tracked them from the Rancho to where they crossed at the Red River, but after that? Yours isn't the only herd traveling through here. Makes it impossible to tell one from the other. Besides, we're not looking for your cattle—I'm taking you to Camp Wichita."

"I know Major Carpenter thought my stepfather's idea was crazy, but what about you? Do you think it's crazy, too?"

"Not really. Scouted that area when I was still in the army. Land there is flat where the Chisholm Trail winds more to avoid the canyons and plateaus. There's several hundred miles of grassland that would provide enough to eat without them losing weight. No, I think the major is wrong. Your stepfather and Lytle had the right idea about that trail.

"The Indians, on the other hand, might not agree. Comanche and Kiowa-Apache hunt this land. Cheyenne too, although their reservation is a couple hundred miles northwest of here."

"Phillips is going to sell them to either the Indians or the army, isn't he?" she asked, already knowing what he would say.

"Probably. Phillips doesn't want any questions about the cattle. I assume your stepfather branded them?"

She nodded. "His initials, JS."

"He's not going to have time to rebrand, so he'll go off trail to avoid the local military. If he's smart, he'll just sell to the Indians."

An unsettled feeling gnawed away at her stomach. She didn't like their odds on this trip. "Maybe Carpenter was right and I am crazy. My luck lately hasn't been good—we'll either not get any help at Camp Wichita, or we'll be attacked by Indians."

Dean slowed his horse until he rode beside her. "Don't talk like that, Miss Anna. Don't tempt fate; it isn't smart. Especially with the problems the military's been having in these parts." He cocked his hat then galloped forward until he was several yards ahead of them.

She frowned. "Is he always that positive?"

"Pretty much."

A hard shudder jerked through her body. She would give just about anything to feel warm again. In the last two days, she hadn't stopped shaking. She could no longer feel her feet as they hung like rocks in the stirrups. "Paul, how much farther until we get to Camp Wichita?"

"If we keep this pace, we could be there tomorrow, maybe by late afternoon."

She bit back a groan. Another night on the plains, freezing. Even the buffalo, with their thick woolly coats, were like ice statues dotting the prairie with mounds of snow resting on their humped backs. She hated winter.

Her memories of her father before he died were vague. She did remember a few special times with him, but couldn't really recall what he looked like, other than dark hair and large hands. She knew from her mother that his family had traveled from Mexico, looking for a better life. She must get her love of the sun from him; how wonderful her skin felt as the heat soaked into her body.

Her stepfather had also been Mexican, but he'd preferred the business end of the ranch and let RJ and the other men tend to matters outside. She still remembered how uncomfortable he'd been the day he'd asked to be her stepfather. They'd driven out to the small pond about a mile from the house and ate a picnic lunch. He'd been so nervous and kept tugging at his shirt collar. She'd grown to love her stepfather, so it had been an easy decision to start using his name as her own.

Her horse pulled his head, startling her out of her reverie. Trying to follow Paul's roan, she pulled back on the reins, forcing her arms to relax. She then realized they were stopping for a quick rest and a bite to eat.

She glanced around the buffalo wallow at the base of a small plateau. The copse of trees surrounding it were scraggly and few. It was a good place to rest and eat. Fifteen or so trees grew close enough together that, even without their leaves, the thick brush stuffed between the skeletal trunks would hide them from the weather and Indians.

Paul broke apart dead branches and started a fire. While the coffee boiled, she took in the surroundings. From her earlier observation, the flat, rolling hills were deceiving. If there were more places like this, she might begin to feel a bit safer.

She hobbled her horse and sat on the fallen tree Dean pulled closer to the fire. Holding the palms of her hands to the hot flames, she relished the wave of heat as it warmed her frozen skin. Inside the copse of winter-dead trees, the harsh wind lessened. Even the horses seemed content, foraging for anything edible.

Paul handed several large chunks of jerked beef to Dean, who sat beside her on the tree trunk. He gave her two smaller pieces. She gnawed on the leather-like meat, enjoying the smoky flavor as her stomach growled again. She started to hold out her hand for a third when a quick movement over his shoulder caught her eye.

Her eyes narrowed as a large black mass appeared, rolling like a wave as it moved over the hills. Jumping to her feet, she yelled, "My cattle!" Before she could grab her horse, Paul's arms wrapped around her, holding her in place beside him.

"Wait, Miss Sanchez—"

She swung around and cut off whatever he was about to say. "I recognize the brindle in the lead. His right horn curls outward at a weird angle. We came up here to get them, and they're right in front of us!"

He jerked her around but continued to hold her against him. "If you'd take the time to look, they aren't being herded by Phillips' men anymore. Those are Comanches. I'm not ready to die, Miss Sanchez, and I don't think you are either. If you go out there, that's what will happen."

From the quick hiss behind them, she knew that Dean had thrown the coffee on the fire, extinguishing the small flames without too much smoke. He then moved to stand beside her.

"You have no right—"

"Yes, I do, Miss Sanchez." Paul's harsh whisper warmed her ear. "I promised the major I'd safely get you to Camp Wichita, and I mean to keep my word. Those warriors have just succeeded in the best raid they've probably had in a while. I'm not going to ride up to them and tell them they have to give you back your cattle."

"In Texas—"

"In Texas you were on a Rancho with many men. Out here you're in their territory, on their terms."

She glared into his face, ignoring his brittle gaze, and clenched her teeth together, knowing he was right. Riding out, just the three of them against fifteen Indians, would get them killed. She growled in frustration—they were so close, and she was miserable. It would only take a few days to get them back to the ranch.

"Fine," she hissed and pulled in a deep breath, stopping mid-breath as she pulled in his scent. Paul smelled like a man who lived outdoors, of wood smoke and fresh air, which soothed her ragged nerves. It disturbed her. She didn't feel like herself—hadn't since she'd been abducted. Before this had all happened, she would never have blindly rushed out into danger.

She sighed, her anger more toward herself than Paul. She was smarter than this, and couldn't help but think her stepfather would be disappointed in her. What was it about this man holding her close with strong arms that brought out the worst in her?

She cleared her throat. "I shouldn't have acted like that. I have no excuse except to say I'm sorry...and thank you." She instantly missed his warmth when he stepped away. A quick glance at the barely visible horizon swallowed up the last three Comanche warriors following her cattle as they disappeared into the falling snow.

She turned around to face the pile of blackened wood that had been their campfire. "Guess I can help by restarting the fire since we didn't get to finish eating..." Her eyes widened and she took a small step back as two men stepped between the trees. One had a dirty bandage wrapped around his head, tufts of sandy brown hair sticking out in places. Even with several feet between them, he smelled as if he'd missed a month of baths.

Paul swung around, his hand going for the gun at his side, thankful he'd taken the loop off when he'd seen the Comanches.

"Stop, mister," the larger of the two said and took another step closer. "Just ease that hand away." He threw a quick glance at Dean who immediately pulled his hand away from his gun.

The man who'd spoken was older, with a touch of gray over his ears. It was hard to tell where his black hair ended and the hat began, he wore it so low on his forehead.

The older man held his gun at hip-level, aimed at Paul's stomach. The stinky man stood a step behind his partner with his palm resting on the handle of his own gun, which was still nestled in the holster.

Paul eased his hand away from the pistol tied against his leg. He moved closer to Anna, using her as a block so they wouldn't see him reaching for the Colt tucked into the back of his pants. Dean took a few steps away from her, his own hand resting on his holstered gun.

"We're no trouble to you. Just let us continue on our way," he said, knowing these men weren't about to let them go. He didn't like the way they were looking at Anna, or the way the younger one kept licking his lips.

"I'm a thinkin' you two boys won't be around much longer, and the pretty lady here will do us just fine. We could use what you have in them saddlebags as well, since those damn Injuns took ours," the younger man said.

Paul's gaze never left the older man. The longer he stared at Anna, the more his gun muzzle dipped. The younger man's attention was also focused on her, and he hadn't yet bothered to draw his gun. Paul knew he wouldn't get another chance.

At this point, all Paul could do was hope Dean followed his lead and shot twice from the hip. The sharp report of Dean's gun sounded at the same time. Paul's first bullet caught the older man in the shoulder and the second tore through his chest. From the force of the impact, the man's arm swung wide and the gun fired into a nearby tree.

Paul glanced at the younger man who was also down, groaning from Dean's bullet. From the wide hole in his stomach, he knew the man wouldn't make it either. "Good job."

Lips pinched together, Dean nodded. "Got your back, sir…er, Paul."

Paul grabbed the food satchel and threw Anna some jerky. "Sorry, but we need to get movin' in case one or two of those Comanches decide to come back and investigate those shots."

Like a true Comanchero, she lifted herself into the saddle. He didn't like how pale her olive complexion had gone, but she waited without a word while he and Dean packed up their small camp.

With a gentle nudge of his boots against the horse's sides, Paul moved to the front of their small group and started them back across the prairie, ignoring the tiny bites as the snow and sleet hit his frozen face. Wanting to stay as far away from the Comanches as possible, he backtracked the herd's trail for several miles then turned northwest toward Camp Wichita.

THE EARLY MORNING sky was still gray as Anna's horse plodded between Paul's and Dean's, repeating the same routine they'd followed over past two days since leaving Texas. They'd ridden for about an hour when Paul held up his hand. Dean and Anna stopped, their horses moving back and forth then stepping sideways in agitation.

"What is it?" Anna asked, pulling her horse up beside his.

Before them, lying amongst the trampled prairie grass, were the bodies of seven men. Most were missing the front of their hair where they'd been scalped, and all were dead. Arrows dotted their chests and their shirtfronts were soaked with blood. She swallowed several times, forcing the bile back down.

"This is horrible," she whispered from behind the palm of her gloved hand. She turned her gaze to the still smoldering chuck wagon. "To die like this…"

"No one deserves this, Miss Anna," Dean said. "I'm afraid we have to leave them. Ground's too hard for burying." He waved his hand along the horizon. "No rocks to cover them with either. When we arrive at Wichita, we'll send some soldiers back."

"Maybe," Paul added. "They won't be able to bury 'em either. They'll probably just leave the bodies here 'til spring, or put them in a cellar until the weather warms up."

She grimaced, looking a bit greener. "How far to Camp Wichita?"

"If the weather doesn't get worse, about three hours." Paul answered.

Spurring her horse, she headed around the carnage with the men following close behind.

Paul had seen Anna's strength after they'd rescued her. Most women he'd known wouldn't have managed half as well as she had on the trail. Most women, that is, except his sister. Megan was one of a kind, and had fought beside him when the Quahadis attacked their wagon train thirteen years before. He'd never met another woman like her—until Anna.

She'd surprised him after they'd killed the two men, remaining poised and strong. He still didn't like having her here. The last thing he needed was to be saddled with a woman, so the sooner he got her to Wichita, the better. The army could deal with Anna Sanchez and her stolen cattle.

From their limited conversations, he recognized her sharp intelligence...yet at the same time she seemed a bit hesitant, as if doubting herself. He watched her talking with Dean, asking him questions and answering his. She gave the kid a wide smile, showing straight, white teeth.

A small flutter filled his chest, and he rubbed his breastbone, trying to rid himself of the uncomfortable feeling. She was indeed beautiful. Instinct told him she was going to be trouble, but he couldn't help the small grin curling his lips. Her smile was infectious.

His grin disappeared as his gaze roamed the seemingly flat land surrounding them. Not only did he worry about protecting the two people with him, but he also knew it was only a matter of time before they ran into more Indians.

These lands were filled with several tribes who refused to stay on the reservation at Camp Wichita. He'd learned how to fight against the Indians' guerrilla-styled warfare after the war, and respected them. In his opinion, there were no better fighters.

Up ahead, a dark silhouette took shape as the military post appeared against the horizon. The craggy peaks of the Wichita Mountain Range rising to the west served as an unusual backdrop to the long, flat buildings spaced out side by side. The landscape was mostly flat, with occasional rolling hills...but something about it called to him.

"It's beautiful, in a bleak sort of way," Anna said, her teeth chattering loud enough for him to hear.

"It is, but we can look tomorrow. For the time being, let's get inside one of those buildings where it's warm." Paul chuckled. "If your teeth chatter much harder, they're gonna break."

He led them into the quadrangle, stopping in front of the white clapboard headquarters building. Dismounting, he tied his horse to the picket post and helped her down, her body stiff from the unrelenting cold. Inside, he grabbed one of the high-backed chairs from its orderly spot against the wall and moved it in front of the fireplace, sitting her on it. The bright orange fire crackled and popped in the good-sized room.

Relieved they'd arrived safely, he glanced around the room, ignoring the sharp tingling of his skin as he warmed up. With only a few other chairs and one desk placed at the far end of the room, the space was sparse. A typical military headquarters.

The young man sitting behind the desk sat up a bit straighter. "May I help you?"

With the back of his hand, Paul brushed the snow off his shoulders then grabbed his hat, slapping it against his leg. Shoving it back on his head, he nodded. "This lady needs to see the man in charge about some cattle stolen by the Comanches."

The soldier moved fast, scurrying through the door adjacent to the desk. After a few quiet minutes, the door reopened, and a man walked out, his boots clomping on the scuffed plank floor.

He was of average size and weight, and his dark brown wavy hair was parted low on one side and slicked back from his high forehead in the current fashion. He had an easy way about him, but at the same time held a quiet power. His sharp gaze told Paul the man missed very little and was seasoned, unlike Dean. Although, he gave the boy credit. He had salt and learned fast...a necessary skill if he stayed in the territory.

The man walked toward them with a relaxed gait and held out one hand, which Paul shook. A small grin formed underneath his heavy mustache and raised the short goatee.

"Lieutenant Colonel John W. Davidson, commanding officer of Camp Wichita. Private Olsen says you're here about some stolen cattle?"

Paul grinned back and gave the commander a quick nod. "Sir, name's Paul Daniels," he held a hand toward his two companions. "Anna Sanchez and Lieutenant Dean Potter. Three days ago, we left a small Rancho near Red River Station on the trail of three thousand head of cattle. Under the orders of a man named Wade Phillips, his men butchered the ranch hands and the owner, then stole the cattle. The man also took Miss Sanchez and kept her prisoner in his home.

"The lieutenant and I were asked to escort Miss Sanchez to you in hopes that you would be able to help her recover her cattle."

Colonel Davidson looked at him from under heavy gray brows then slowly laid the pen he still held on the desk. "Sorry, Mr. Daniels, but I don't have the manpower to help you. I'm waiting on new recruits. Seems I'm to corral Indians with a bunch of greenhorns."

Dean stepped forward and gave the colonel a quick salute then stood at attention.

"Lieutenant?"

"Sir, a couple of hours ago, about ten miles south of here, we saw a small group of Comanches—I counted fifteen—pushin' the herd west. About two miles farther north of where we saw them, we came across the bodies of the men who stole the cattle from Miss Sanchez's ranch."

Davidson's scowled. "Damned Indians are going to be the death of me."

Paul stared at the colonel a moment, not quite believing what he'd heard. "Sir, I think the more important issue is making sure Phillips doesn't come after Miss Sanchez again."

"You're right, you're right, sorry. You said the cows were originally stolen in Texas?"

"Yes, sir."

Davidson picked up his pen and grabbed a sheet of paper and started writing. "I'm sending a letter to Fort Phantom Hill. Since this event happened in Texas, Texans will have to take care of it."

CHAPTER 5

Returning from the mess hall with everyone's coffee, Anna gave the young officer who closed the front door of the headquarters building behind her a small smile. She set the tin tray on the desk and the steaming cups in front of the men as her two companions continued to talk to the colonel. More accurately, as the colonel talked and Paul and Dean listened.

The early morning greeted them with clear blue skies, but the temperature was still below freezing. She shivered. Even inside, tendrils of icy air seeped between the door and the frame of the building.

She gave Dean a quick glance, his young face filled with youthful admiration for the commanding officer. She looked over at Paul, who stared in concentration at whatever Colonel Davidson was saying.

Paul's dark brown eyebrows drew together in a serious frown. Even scowling, he was very handsome. But the way he moved surprised her. Every motion was precise and fluid, nothing wasted. He reminded her of a cat…or an Indian.

She forced herself to concentrate on the conversation

instead of the way he filled out the black trousers better than most men she'd seen. Or the way his shirt sleeves tightened over his arm muscles. A tingle of excitement filled her chest, knowing how improper her thoughts were. She couldn't help but wonder what it would feel like to have his arms wrapped around her. She grinned at the thought of her mother's horrified reaction if she could see inside her head.

Her smile disappeared when Davidson mentioned a small spread not far from the newly constructed camp, somewhere inside the Wichita Mountains to the northwest. Evidently, they weren't done traveling, and she couldn't help feeling a bit vexed at the idea of climbing back onto a horse and trudging through the snow-covered plains. It didn't matter how bad she wanted the cattle. They'd just arrived and, for the first time in three days, she was warm.

"...can get there by nightfall. The ranch is owned by a man familiar to both the military and the Comanches," Davidson said. "How he managed to gain their trust is a mystery, although I normally wouldn't set store by the trust of an Indian. The Comanche change as fast as the weather here in this godforsaken prairie. However, I do trust his judgment. He's canny and knows people. If anyone can help retrieve your stolen cattle, it's Flores."

"Captain Ricardo Flores?" Paul asked.

"The same. Not many men like him left."

Paul nodded. "We served together under Davis in the Third Division at the siege of Corinth then in the Fourteenth Division, XIII Corps under General Benton. We followed him to Alabama, the Battle of Fort Blakely."

Ricardo Flores...that was her father's name. She frowned. His was a common enough name. She'd heard of other men with the same name back in Texas, but it still made her pause. Her mother had lied to her before, betraying her trust.

Would she have lied about this too? Could her father still be alive?

She fingered the small golden locket nestled in the hollow of her throat. They'd planned to have their pictures taken so she could put them inside. Turning eight years old had been bittersweet. He'd given her the locket after her birthday party. Several days later, her mother told her and her brother that he was dead. She didn't have a single picture of her father to remember him by.

"Anna?" Paul's worried gaze met hers. "Is something wrong?"

She forced her head from side to side. Until she knew for sure who this man was, she wouldn't say anything. "No. Just a bit tired and hungry."

AFTER BREAKFAST, Anna felt restless. Instead of retiring to her room, she walked out to the barn. Being near the animals had always calmed her nerves, mostly when she'd been younger and fighting with her mother. The repetitive motion of brushing her horse's mottled brown coat was soothing, but only momentary as her thoughts returned to her mother.

Try as she might, she couldn't figure out her mother's motive for giving her to Phillips…until she remembered the last time she and her mother argued. Anna's hand paused, the brush resting against the horse's neck as she replayed the conversation in her mind.

Her mother sipped her coffee from the delicate pink porcelain cup. "I've decided to sell the Rancho and return home. You will be coming with me. You should be married with children of your own. You're twenty-five—a spinster!"

Anna leaned against the chair's high back, ignoring the slight cracking of the joints. "But, I don't want to leave, Mama. I want to someday run the Rancho. Besides, if I ever do marry, it will be for love."

Her mother clinked the cup on the table, laced her fingers together, and placed them in her lap, her cold blue gaze never wavering. "There is no such thing as love, young lady. Either you return with me, or you will be married." She rose, slowly walking to the door.

Stopping in the doorway, her mother barely turned her head, never looking back into the room and added, "You forced my hand, Anna. If you insist on disregarding my wishes, you will *marry."*

The argument was an old one—one her mother threatened every time she disagreed with her. She let out a deep breath, not knowing whether to scream or cry. Her mother had all but told her what she was going to do, but Anna hadn't listened.

She thought back to her favorite memory—the last birthday she'd had with her father. How she missed those simple times. To celebrate her turning eight, he'd taken her into town for a special dinner. On their way home, he'd given her his present; the gold necklace she still wore. He'd picked her up and twirled her around, telling her that no matter what, he would always be there for her.

Pulling the brush through the horse's mane, she let out a soft sigh. It had been a stupid promise, but she loved that he'd made it anyway.

She'd never understood her mother, and had always been closer to her father and her brother, who was two years her junior. She and her brother had done everything together until he'd run off to fight in the War Between the States. Richard had only been fourteen. He, too, had promised to always be there for her.

She'd kept her little brother's promise alive in her heart—until he'd been killed. She still prayed every night he was safe—that somehow the report of her brother's death had been a mistake and he would come home. But as the years went by without any word from him, she knew he was dead. Her brother would never do that to her.

"In this weather, that horse is gonna need his hair."

Startled, she jerked around to see Paul standing inside the stable, his arms crossed over his chest and a small grin turning up one side of his mouth. Glancing back at where she'd been brushing, she felt her cheeks burn. She didn't like being caught unawares…but with everything running through her mind at full speed, he'd been able to sneak up on her.

"I'm sure there's a logical explanation for why you're brushing the hair right off that poor pony. Not used to havin' a female around anymore, but I think I can remember how to listen. If you'd like."

She tossed the brush on the ground near the stall's short wall, wrapped her arm under the horse's neck, and scratched the stubbly hairs along the jaw. Studying Paul's face, she took a deep breath, enjoying the blend of scents within the barn: hay, leather, and horse…but wished she could smell the man instead.

"So, you really fought in the war?"

"I did. Like I told Davidson, I fought for the Union. Served with Captain Flores, the man we're goin' to see. Cap was what we called him. I joined up because, for me, it was the right thing to do. For Cap, well, his father got caught in the Missouri uprisings along with his wife's family. After his parents were killed, he joined the military. Seemed natural for him to side with the Union. He's a good man and my friend. Saved each other's lives several times over. If anybody can help get your cattle back, it's him."

This man didn't sound like her father at all. The war hadn't started until she was thirteen. Her father would never have left without a word...maybe her mother hadn't lied to her after all?

"Do you know why he settled here and never returned to Missouri? Did he have any siblings?" She met his green gaze. "I can't imagine staying away from one's family on purpose. Then again, I'm not a man."

"No, ma'am, you definitely aren't. I don't know why he came here or if he was an only child or not. After the war, we went separate ways."

She met his smile. "I guess I can understand that. After my father died, my mother, brother, and I traveled a lot. Sometimes even now, I'd like nothing more than to just get on my horse and ride away. I love the ranch and can't imagine living anywhere else—I'd even miss helping with the cattle. But to travel again... I guess you never really get the wanderlust out of your system once it's there."

"No, you don't." He raised one eyebrows. "You really helped with the cattle?"

She nodded. "I like putting my stepfather's brand on them. The first few times, I thought I was going to be sick from the odor of singed hair and burning flesh, but I got used to it. I was proud of what I did for my stepfather."

"Like a son?"

She smiled. "Yes, like a son."

Closing her eyes, she tried to stop the aching fury coursing through her. "How could she be so cruel? My mother is so self-centered—look at what she's done. Just so she could return to New Orleans without the scandal of another divorce! Her actions have killed so many men." She stared at her hands still resting against the horse.

"She's left me with nothing—no family, no home. Nothing!" Her voice raised, sounding shrill in her own ears, but she couldn't seem to stop talking. Counting slowly to ten in her mind, she took deep, even breaths, trying to calm herself down. "How could she be so self-serving?" she asked in a small whisper.

She wrapped her coat tight around her and dropped her head, staring at the straw-covered ground, feeling drained and furious at the same time...and not knowing how to stop any of it.

"I'm sorry. I don't usually act like this, but..." She let out a frustrated growl. "I need some coffee. If you don't mind putting up with my foul mood, would you like to join me?"

Instead of waiting for an answer, she took off at a brisk walk across the compound toward the mess hall. Inside the somewhat warmer room, she poured a little cream and sugar into her coffee and sat at one of the long tables. Paul, sitting across from her, sipped his drink. She could never drink her coffee black like he did, and was thankful the military didn't skimp on the cream and sugar.

"So, what about you? Where's your family?"

He set the half empty cup on the table, cradling it between his hands, two fingers from each hand twined through the handle. For several minutes he didn't say a word.

"I'm sorry, it's none of my business."

His sad, green eyes tugged at her heart, and she wondered what had happened to him. One corner of his mouth rose as if he tried to smile.

"No, it's fine. I grew up in Colorado, the youngest of four: two brothers and one sister."

"You're lucky. My brother died during the war. The past nine years that he's been gone have been lonely. I've learned to carry on great conversations with myself or my animals. I'll admit though, they are rather one-sided and boring."

This time, he smiled. "And you said I was strange?"

Her cheeks warmed. She'd fallen right into that one. It was nice to hear him joke. He always seemed to be so serious and quiet. She pressed her lips together and bit back a chuckle. Her stepfather always told her she'd never learn to think before saying something. The thought of her stepfather—his murder—shriveled the tiny moment of happiness.

PAUL STARED INTO HIS COFFEE, swirling the dark brown liquid. Anna made a noise low in her throat, pulling his gaze to her face. Her expression went from happy to worried. Or was it sad? He couldn't really tell. She sipped her drink, her gaze staring at a spot on the table between them. He couldn't help but wonder what her thoughts were.

He understood her worry as she tried to piece together her life. What he didn't understand was why he wanted to help her. He could've just left her here and been on his way. But for some reason, he couldn't turn his back on her.

His gaze followed the gentle slope of her cheek, running along her narrow jaw then down her long, elegant neck before moving back up to her rich brown eyes.

She met his gaze then glanced back down at the cup gripped between her hands. "I just don't understand. What she did was no different than selling me to the highest bidder. Why would she give me to that heinous man? She knew how he was—all the trouble he'd caused us."

She wiped a stray tear from her cheek. "I'd like to think she didn't realize he was a murderer, but..." Her eyes widened. "Maybe Phillips just made everything up?" She jerked to a stand, the chair legs clattering as they wobbled on the floor. "I'm sorry. You don't need to hear any of this." She rose and turned to leave but stopped when he said her name.

"Try to remember not everything is always as it seems."

She stared at him a moment then left the building. He gulped the last swallow of coffee and glanced longingly at the dented coffeepot. He didn't have time for another cup if they were going to reach the mountains by nightfall.

Paul packed their gear in record time then headed toward the headquarters building. Pulling the heavy door open, he stepped inside and the cold wind slammed the door shut behind him. Instead of the colonel or his aide, another soldier sat behind the desk, unmoving as Paul walked toward him.

"Just wanted to tell the colonel thank you for his help before we left."

"I'm afraid he's indisposed at the moment. You're going to have to change your plans, at least for tonight. Another storm heading in. Should hit within the hour. I'd hate if, in your eagerness to leave, you'd put Miss Sanchez's life in danger."

The door opened behind Paul, letting in another cold blast of wind which did nothing to stem his rising anger. He didn't like this arrogant man.

"Oh, there you are. Dean's looking for you." Anna walked around him and stopped, the slow smile she gave the man aggravating Paul even more.

Paul watched as he moved around the desk and raised Anna's hand to his lips. The anger suddenly flooding through his body surprised him as he reminded himself that he was only here to escort her on to Captain Flores's house.

As they talked, he took the time to look the man over. He was a few inches shorter than his own six feet, with a body thin enough a strong breeze would blow him over. He had close-set, pale blue eyes that held no warmth, thin lips, and a crooked nose. Sticking out from underneath his cap was shaggy blond hair that hadn't seen scissors in several months.

He'd seen many men like this soldier during the war. This man held himself aloof with a self-important air. Paul noticed his hand never strayed from the pistol he wore high on his hip. This soldier reminded him of the men he'd met farther west, those who liked to shoot first and talk last.

Anna held up her palm toward him. "I see you've met my escort?" At the slight shake of his head, she told him Paul's name. She gave the sergeant an embarrassed smile. "I'm sorry, but I didn't catch your name."

The man's cold gaze briefly touched on Paul's face then refocused on Anna. "I am Sergeant John Taylor." He gave her a slight bow, immediately dismissing Paul. "Ma'am, since the weather has delayed your trip until the morning, would you allow me to escort you to supper?"

Her smile widened when Taylor raised his elbow, and she wound her arm through his.

Paul stared at the closed door for several minutes after they'd left. The man seemed familiar, but he couldn't remember where he might have seen him before.

CHAPTER 6

Sometime during the early morning hours the snow let up, making travel a bit easier. Still, even Dean agreed with Anna that he wasn't eager to leave the warmth and comfort the buildings provided.

As the day progressed, they made good time. The sun warmed their skin as the miles passed by, and the terrain grew hillier as they drew closer to the small mountain range. That evening, they camped in a buffalo hollow, which gave them little protection from the increasing wind. But it was better than nothing.

With only three, maybe four miles to go before they reached the area Colonel Davidson described, another storm hit. Dark clouds sifted to the ground and covered everything in a heavy gray mist. The horses slipped and stumbled in the mounting snow. Hunched over on their mounts, sleet pelted them from what seemed like all directions.

Paul was glad when Davidson ordered Dean to continue with them until they reached Flores' small spread. He liked the kid and was glad for the male company, even if none of them talked much.

From underneath the brim of his hat, which didn't help much, the icy pellets slapped him in the face as he tried to make out any familiar landmarks. Ahead, he could just make out the hazy dark outline of the Wichita Mountains as they drew closer.

If the storm didn't let up, they weren't going to make the ranch, much less find it. He kept his eyes busy, always moving from side to side, looking for anything they could use as shelter. They had only traveled a couple of miles, but the horses weren't going to be able to keep this up much longer. What they needed was a cave. Even a small grotto would work as long, as it provided some protection. Otherwise the horses would freeze to death.

"Paul!" Dean hollered over the wailing winds. The young man pointed to a grouping of snow-covered trees looming out of the surrounding whiteness. The trunk of a large tree leaned against a red cedar growing a few feet away and made a sort of door into what Paul hoped was shelter.

He walked his horse into the trees, and the swirling snow-laden wind died off. The trees stood close together and were covered in brambles and vines, providing a natural barrier against the elements for them and the horses. Several huge rocks had fallen on top of each other forming a primitive arch, but at least it protected them from the frigid winds.

They climbed down from the horses, and with Dean's help, got them unsaddled and rubbed down as best they could. Turning them loose, he knew they wouldn't go far from what little wild grass and foliage the snow hadn't covered.

"Let's hope this snowstorm clears out soon. There's not enough foliage to feed the horses for longer than a day, maybe two if we're lucky," Dean said.

Paul picked up the blanket from Anna's horse and placed it around her hunched shoulders. Even with the heavy coat, her body was shaking. He added a few more logs to the fire and held his palms above the flickering orange flames. As warmth returned, sharp tingles spread from the tips of his fingers and into his wrists like a million wasp stings. It took several minutes, but the pain disappeared as his hands thawed. He warmed himself a bit longer then started a pot of water boiling for coffee.

He poured three cups and handed Anna hers. "Sugar?"

She nodded without saying anything, which worried him. Since beginning this journey, she'd asked questions and talked...but not too much. Which was good, because there was nothing worse than someone who could never be quiet. However, her silence didn't bode well either, and he hoped a hot cup of coffee would bring her back to herself.

He wished he knew why the Rancho was so important to her. Trying to drive cattle in such a harsh winter was asking for problems. Summer drives were difficult enough with stiff muscles from long days in the saddle and unending nights where your only companion was a horse and a thousand winking stars overhead.

Winter drives were far worse, with added freezing temperatures. Man and beast stayed frozen from the frigid prairie winds until warmth became nothing more than an elusive dream.

"Why is the Rancho so important to you? Driving cattle anywhere right now isn't smart. No ranch is worth your life."

Her eyes never left the fire. Never acknowledged him. She sat unmoving except for the twisting of the blanket between her fingers.

"Anna?"

At the sound of her name, a warm sensation filled her, easing some of the tension and the tight feeling in her chest. With the corners of her blanket gripped in each fist, she crossed her arms over her chest and pulled it tighter. As if that was all she needed to hold the warmth in and thaw her frozen heart.

If Anna were being truthful to herself, she would admit that she didn't want to be here anymore. She wanted to return to Texas and her small world. She wished she was sitting comfortably in front of the large fireplace in their great room and sipping Maria's coffee with a bit of added cacao bean powder. No one made better coffee than the grandmotherly cook. She missed her advice, and hoped that somehow, she'd escaped everyone else's fate back on the ranch.

She pushed back her shoulders, resolution filling her mind. This whole mess was going to work itself out. The Rangers would succeed in arresting Phillips, and she would get the deed back to her home. And somehow, she was going to get her cattle back from the Comanche.

She thought about Paul's question. He knew her relationship with her mother wasn't good, thanks to her falling apart in front of him in the barn. How could she describe the mercurial emotions between her and her mother or all the loss of those she loved? How could she explain what she herself didn't understand?

She raised her head, its weight heavy on her neck, which was sore and pinched from riding hunched over her horse for most of the day. She tipped her head to one side, letting the muscles stretch out, then repeated with the other side.

Wondering how to respond to his question, she studied his face. She never tired of looking at him. He was boyishly handsome. His brown hair brushed against the top of his shirt collar; longer than now fashionable, but it suited him.

His skin still held the hint of a tan from months in the sun, but it was his eyes drawing her, pulling at her heart. They never stayed still, taking in everything around him. Their light green filled her mind with pictures of lush meadows in early summer. Of course, they also reminded her how cold she was.

"Anna?" Paul asked again. "Please answer me. Why is the Rancho so important to you?"

She heard the worry in his voice, and her insides tingled. She liked hearing him say her name. "After my father died, we moved around a lot. When Jonathan Sanchez married my mother and we moved to the Rancho, I felt like I was home. Out of my mother's three other husbands, he put up with her the longest—almost ten years.

"It's the only home I've ever really known. I only want to get the herd back so all my stepfather's hard work building the Rancho isn't for naught. Just before we left Camp Wichita, Sergeant Taylor suggested I try to sell a part of the herd to the army instead of trying to get them back home again. Either way," She threw her hands up, glancing toward the sky. "They're going to be nothing but skin and bones, which will do me no good."

Paul reached over and grabbed one of the thicker branches. He threw it on top of the fire and waited as it spit and popped. "You're right. This winter's settin' up to be harsh." After a moments' pause, he continued. "Tell me 'bout your brother. What happened to him?"

She pulled the blanket tighter around her shoulders and squirmed, the rock hard and uncomfortable beneath her. "He was my best friend. I was so afraid when he left to fight in the war, but as the months wore on his absence got a bit easier. After he died, I even hated him for a while." She frowned at him across the fire. "Does that make me a terrible person?"

Paul shook his head. "Makes you human."

She shrugged. "I've told myself that, but it doesn't make it any easier."

"If they don't catch Phillips, what're you goin' to do about the Rancho?" Paul poured himself another cup of coffee, emptying the rest into hers, and started a new pot.

She shook her head. "I don't know. The Rangers can only handle so much, and the area they protect is too big for one group to manage. If they can't find Phillips..."

"There are soldiers at Red River Station and Fort Phantom Hill."

She raised an eyebrow. "The military in Texas is not too helpful with civilian problems. They only step in when ordered to." She stared at the bouncing flames, anxiety eating away at her. She didn't have a lot of options, and that terrified her.

He added several twigs and another smaller branch to the fire. "Not surprising. Even though it's been eight years since the war ended, states are still tryin' to recover."

She glanced up as Dean scurried down the slippery rocks and slid to a quick stop a few inches behind Paul, his outstretched arms circling in wide circles as he fought for balance. He looked so ridiculous she couldn't help but laugh. Laughing felt good.

Dean leaned over beside Paul's head and whispered, his soft-spoken words unintelligible. Paul's gaze sharpened, his eyes turning an icy green. He stood and grabbed his rifle and pistol. "Stay here and don't move. Keep your gun close and ready."

"What? Why?"

He leaned toward her, his face a tight mask. "If we're lucky, we may just get Phillips now. Just stay here!"

She gasped, her eyes widening. "He's here? Now?" Her voice hissed in a tight whisper.

Paul nodded, then climbed out of the rocky enclosure with Dean on his tail, leaving her alone. A hard knot formed in her stomach, and a frisson of fear skittered through her, raising the tiny hairs on her arms and neck.

Nervously, she pulled her rifle from the scabbard, checking to make sure it was loaded before laying it across her lap. She also reached inside the saddlebag and grabbed her Smith & Wesson revolver and a box of cartridges, laying them on the ground beside her.

To calm her nerves, she inhaled the subtle scent of oak from the fire. The small chunks of wood were dry, so there was very little smoke. Not that it mattered in the heavy snow falling around them.

The sharp staccato of gunfire echoed somewhere close by. She grabbed the pistol and held her breath until her chest ached, saying a little prayer that Paul and Dean were okay. The whine of another bullet went over her head and hit the rocks just behind her, sending a shower of razor-like splinters of granite down on her.

Ducking, she covered her head, but not before hearing what she thought was her name. Holding still, she waited and heard it again. The voice sounded familiar, but it was too faint. Jerking her head around, she tried to see past the rocky ledges above her, but the falling snow was too thick.

"Anna..."

With the wind howling through the trees, she almost didn't hear the faint voice. She glanced around, looking for Paul or Dean.

"Anna Elizabeth..."

"Where are you, Phillips! You coward!" She twisted around, trying to see where he was.

"Are you ready to go home, Anna?"

From the sound of his voice, Phillips had inched closer, but she still had no idea where he was. Her heart stuttered, and she froze as fear paralyzed her limbs. She forced her eyes to blink as the rocks on the other side of the grotto wavered then doubled.

Where was Paul?

She stood, the pistol clutched in her tight fist and stepped closer to the fire. Turning, she aimed the gun at several overhangs and other places a person might try to hide on the mountainside.

Phillips wrapped one arm around her and pulled her against him, covering her mouth and nostrils with his gloved hand. Jerking from side to side, she twisted her body, trying to free herself and didn't see the second man until he jerked her gun from her hand.

"Stay still, my sweet. I don't want you to hurt yourself. It wasn't very nice of you to leave my home, and now you have the Texas police looking for me too. This time, however, I'm going to make sure you don't get away."

Too mad to be afraid, she screamed her denial, but her muffled curses only sounded like grunts and mumbles against his hand as she clawed at him. Black dots appeared in her vision, and her lungs felt like they were going to explode.

"Be a good girl, like your dear mother raised you to be, and shut up. By now, your two friends are dead, and if not? Well, they soon will be."

He dropped his hand from her face and she gasped, dragging in the cold air in deep, gulping breaths. Her head fell forward and she closed her eyes, refusing to believe they were gone.

"There are twenty-two men surrounding your little camp," Phillips said. "So you see, my sweet, it is quite hopeless for you." He pinched her chin between his fingers and jerked her face back up to meet his. "But you must promise not to scream. It will do you no good, and I hate loud noises."

He waited until she nodded then removed his arms. Before she could move away from him, a rope encircled her, pinning her arms to her sides. She let out her pent-up fury in a loud scream, sick and tired of always looking over her shoulder because of this man.

Before she could gather enough air for another scream, he pulled her close. The hungry leer in his eyes made her stomach turn over in a summersault. Pulling her head away, she couldn't hide her contempt. Everything he'd done to her and her family boiled up from the deep well inside where she'd pushed it, nourishing and feeding every bad thought she'd had. Fury blended in with her fear, giving her the courage to spit in his face.

No longer did she think him passably handsome as his face twisted into an ugly grimace. His lips curled down in disgust as he wiped the spittle from his cheek in a jerky thrust. His eyes narrowed and, before she could react, he slapped her. The sharp sting of his palm against her cold skin burned like fire.

"Do not test my patience, my dear. You won't like the punishment."

He jammed a rag between her lips and tied it at the back of her neck. Grabbing her by the arms, he shoved her onto the rocky shelf behind them. She rolled away from the ledge just as he pulled himself up beside her. She grunted when another pair of hands jerked her upright.

"You won't get away with this," she mumbled through the nasty-tasting material, thankful it wasn't too tight.

One side of his mouth rose in an evil sneer. "Who's going to stop me? You? I doubt that." He motioned with a flick of his hand to whoever held her and added, "Get her saddled up."

She glared, twisting and trying to drag her heels as the man holding her forced her backward. "I will kill you for this," she hissed at him. As the man hefted her on the horse, the sound of Phillips' laughter faded into the wailing wind.

CHAPTER 7

Paul stared at the scene below him. After the initial attack, he and Dean managed to work their way around their small camp, picking off several of Phillips' men as they tried to surround them. In one hand, he held his Bowie knife and in the other, his Colt. His rifle lay empty beside him on the overhang.

He remained motionless and listened. Slowly, he crawled to the rocky overhang as silently as possible. Close by, a boot scuffed against rock. A second later came a soft hiss. He twisted on his back, his gun out in front of him.

A dark form edged closer, and he took up the slack on the trigger and waited.

"Paul?" Dean whispered, dropping into a tight crouch.

"Hell, boy, you almost got yourself shot." He rolled back on his stomach to keep his eye on Anna when she spit in Phillips' face. He clenched his jaws, mentally promising himself to make Phillips suffer when he caught up with him. "Girl's got spirit, I'll give her that."

Dean crawled beside him, a gun in each hand, and a

bloody scratch running along the side of his right hand. "What'd she do?"

"Spit in his face. Probably not the smartest thing she could've done, cuz now he's furious. Still, gotta admire her." He held himself still when the slap against her cheek echoed in his ears. "He's going to pay for doing that."

"Damn straight," Dean agreed. "What do you think he's planning to do with her?"

"Take her back to Texas, I reckon." He glanced at the three riders waiting at the bottom of the mountain when five more rode up to join them. One was slumped forward against his horse's neck. "How many did you get?"

"Five. You?"

"Eight." He jutted his chin toward the men. "Ninth seems to be a mite injured. Got up close and personal-like with my knife. Didn't want to risk shootin' you too."

Dean gave him a crooked grin. "Thanks, I think. I saw you tracking a couple of them to my south, so I headed a bit more to the north to make sure. How many are still out there, you think?"

Paul shrugged. "It's any man's guess, but I'm hopin' that's all of 'em down there."

"They're moving out. What do you want to do?"

From their perch, they watched the horses gingerly pick their way down off the rocky slope. Paul didn't like this situation one bit. He was tired of fighting, which was why he'd left the army. He didn't search out trouble, but somehow always managed to find himself in the middle of a fight. He'd tempted lady luck several times during his life, and he wasn't sure how many more times she was going to let him scrape by.

Left to die as a child, he'd been found and raised by a good family. After being shot during a Comanche attack, he'd been saved by a Caddo elder. The last time had been in the war, when Captain Flores rescued him from a Confederate ambush.

If he didn't think of something quick, any chance of rescuing Anna would become very slim. They were outnumbered, and the weather wasn't helping either. He pulled his coat collar up underneath the brim of his hat to keep the snowflakes from landing on the back of his neck.

He knew bringing Anna here would end in trouble, and now they had it. What had happened to finding a stretch of land, building a small house, and breeding horses? He'd had his fill of punching cattle. He'd never had anything he could call his own. For the last eight years, he'd ridden the line, herding cattle up the Chisholm Trail from Texas to Kansas. It had been hard work, and he'd even managed to put back some wages…but not enough to amount to much.

He eased back from the rocky ledge and sat on his heels. "Not too much we can do in this storm. We can try to stay close and hope they don't see us, but if the snow doesn't let up, we won't be goin' anywhere easily. There's no way to get her before they get us."

"And we have no idea if there are more men close by either." Dean peered out from underneath the brim of his hat with narrowed eyes. "We could also just wait until they camp for the night."

"We'll lose too much time, and the snow will cover their tracks. Besides, they may not stop."

"They might. From their positions on the ground, they wouldn't know there were cutouts in the large rocks where we could hide. They probably think they got us with the barrage of bullets they unloaded. If we're lucky, they won't be expecting anyone on their tail."

Paul shook his head. His gut told him they needed to stay as close as they could without giving away that they were in the ravine behind them. "We follow 'em."

Patting the roan's neck, he saddled his horse, thankful they'd found the hidden grotto farther up the mountain. Otherwise, they'd be walkin'. He brushed snow from the leather seat and stepped into the stirrup. Together, he and Dean made their way down to the now empty camp.

They found the tracks rapidly filling in with snow, and followed as fast as their horses could through the thick drifts. Before long, however, they caught up. Unfortunately, the snowstorm was letting up. They fell farther behind so they wouldn't be spotted by anyone in the group up ahead. He glanced at the mountain behind. They were still northwest of Camp Wichita, but the going was slow.

Their camp was a good one, tucked at the bottom of a shallow arroyo, the walls high enough to protect against the winds. He'd heard stories about this area. The prairie was rutted with these shallow crevices, cut deep into the heart by ancient rivers.

After eating a quick bite of hardtack and jerky, he scouted around and found Phillips' camp not too far from theirs in an almost adjacent ravine. Knowing there was nothing he could do, he made his way back to where Dean waited with the horses.

"How're we getting her back?" Dean stared at him, nursing his cup of coffee between his palms.

Paul threw a few more branches on the fire and sat back, pulling his blanket up to his chest. "Not rightly sure at the moment, but a plan will come to me eventually."

Dean's brows drew together in a worried frown. "Before daybreak?"

He closed his eyes and rested his head against his saddle, forcing his tight muscles to relax, which wasn't easy. The only thought in his mind was to saddle up again and find Anna before something worse happened to her. "We'll head out at first light. We'll get her back—that's a promise."

. . .

MORNING DAWNED COLD AND STILL. The sky slowly lightened, bleeding shades of pinks and oranges as the sun rose. Anna couldn't feel her arms anymore. Phillips had kept the rope tied around her during the night. She'd tossed and turned, lying awake most of the night wondering where Paul and Dean were. Why hadn't they rescued her yet?

Her jaw popped from the force of her yawn. A bear of a man lifted her to the saddle, keeping hold of the reins while he saddled up.

They followed the gully, which wound through the earth like a snake, curling back and forth as it made its way southeast. Riding along the sandy bottom offered a nice reprieve from the cold winds above. Dotting the rock walk were dark, icy patches, which she knew indicated underground seepage of water.

"How far does this run?" she asked the man beside her.

He shrugged. "Not sure and don't care."

She stared at him. "You don't really think you're going to get away with this, do you?"

The man stared straight ahead, every once in a while leaning away and spitting, the black tobacco juice splattering against the canyon wall.

She knew somewhere behind them were Paul and Dean. That knowledge gave her courage. Glancing around at the men, she knew she'd never seen any of them before. She considered her options and didn't like any of them…until she saw the man beside her and the untied gun on his left hip.

Eventually they would have to exit the winding arroyo, and above them was open prairie with nowhere to hide. She needed to come up with a plan before that happened. Anything to give the boys a chance to catch up before one of the scouts Phillips had sent out earlier spotted them.

Her captors pressed on until early afternoon, the only sounds were the soft footfalls of their horses on the packed earth. Rounding another bend, she jumped when a loud voice overhead called out.

"Rangers are close, Mr. Phillips! I jus' spotted them comin' this way from the southeast, headin' straight fer us!"

"Dad-blasted devils! We continue with my plan."

She curled her upper lip in disgust at the haughtiness in his voice. He held himself erect in the saddle, the reins dangling loosely through his limp hand.

"If they find us with that girl..." the scout snarled, turning his head a little to spit on the snow. "We need to get shut of her. This was a stupid idea. If them police catch up to us, we'll hang."

"Shut up, Jensen! When I want your opinion, I'll ask for it."

A loud shot echoed around them, followed by a heavy silence. Anna forced her gaze from the revolver in Phillips' hand to the man he'd called Jensen. She gagged, quickly turning away and throwing up. Closing her eyes, the image of the man's head was burned into her mind; the bloody, jagged shards of his skull outlining the large hole in the back of his head, a steady trickle of blood dripping from the wound to the dirt floor below.

"Now," Phillips said in a cold, commanding voice. "If anyone would like to add something to Mr. Jensen's objections?" Thirty seconds passed without a response. "I didn't think so—."

Without thinking, Anna lunged for the pearl-handled pistol resting untied in the large man's holster. Raising it, she thumbed back the hammer and pulled the trigger. The man's eyes widened in shock as he stared down at her, his mouth falling open as he slid from his horse, hitting the ground with a *thud*.

Phillips fought for control of his horse which had twisted around, startled by the gun's loud report. He shouted out to his men, alarm and shock on his face. "Hold the girl! Tom, grab the rope before—"

Her own mount backed up a few feet then sidestepped as one of the men turned in his saddle and fired. She swung the gun toward Phillips and fired again. Another shot rang out then two more, sounding muted and far away as she watched Phillips' lifeless body hang from his saddle then drop to the ground.

A rush of cold flooded her insides as she stared into his lifeless eyes.

FEARING they were too late and Anna had been shot, Paul slapped his heels against his horse and lunged forward. He pulled up short as they rode into a space big enough to fit a small cabin, his gun drawn. Dean rode up beside him, his rifle pointing at the two men still on horseback across from them.

"Hold your fire, boys. We've got 'em covered."

Paul glanced upward and saw a line of Rangers along the top edge of the ravine—the same men who helped rescue Anna the first time.

"Seems to me, you've had a hard time keepin' this little filly out of trouble." Major Carpenter stared down at them. He pulled on the brim of his hat and added a quick, "Ma'am."

Anna still sat on the ground, her legs outstretched in front of her. A well-built appaloosa stood over her. On the ground not two feet away sat a man, holding his head in his hands and moaning. Beside him lay a second man, his coat and shirt covered in blood.

Paul dropped from his horse and walked toward her, squatting by her side. "Anna?"

She jerked at the sound of his voice but continued staring at the body in front of her. Without taking his eyes off of her, he asked in a quiet voice, "Phillips?"

She slowly nodded.

He stared hard at the body, dark brown eyes staring sightlessly at the blue sky, a small hole in the center of his forehead, and three more bullet holes had torn through the leather of the man's coat.

"Nice shootin', Miss Sanchez. But I think my men can take it from here," Carpenter said.

She frowned and lifted the pearl-handled pistol still gripped in a tight fist, staring at it as if she'd never seen it before. "That man," she nodded to the one holding his bloody side. "He had RJ's gun. I took it..."

Paul wrapped his hand around hers and gently pulled the gun from her tight grip, tucking it behind his front waistband, then turned to the major. "How'd you know we were here?"

"Didn't. Heard a gunshot and figured it came from the arroyo. Land's a might open and flat to hide someone, so this was the most obvious place to search." He motioned toward two familiar soldiers, Smith and Corbin, who moved their horses forward. "Keep a sharp eye on the prisoners."

They stayed up top while the rest of Carpenter's men made their way down by way of an almost invisible narrow ledge running down the side of the wall. They collected the guns and tied the two men still alive onto the back of their horses. Each policeman grabbed a set of reins and led the men and extra horses back up the ledge.

"We followed Phillips and his men north. We stopped by Camp Wichita and learned you were headed this way," Carpenter said. "Figured to warn you. If you're still goin' to Flores's ranch, stay in the ravine. He'll be glad to see you though. Needs as much help as he can get. Ornery ol' cuss won't leave his place. Someone's out to cause him problems and took almost half his herd along with quite a few of his horses. What few men he had helping him were killed too."

ANNA HEARD their conversation as if in a dream, listening to the major as he gave instructions to his men. A minute later, she heard the steady plodding of the horses' hooves against the hard-baked earth as they were led out of the ravine.

She heard Paul's voice, the sound soothing, thawing some of the icy chill from her limbs. She tried to focus, listening to his words without understanding them. She felt a gentle pressure on her shoulder then a small shake, which jiggled her head back and forth.

"Ma'am?" Carpenter asked. "You all right?"

Anna nodded, her gaze locked on the body lying on the ground in front of her. Her stomach heaved again, but she clamped her lips together, refusing to throw up in front of them. Her body was numb, her heart heavy. She'd just killed a man.

CHAPTER 8

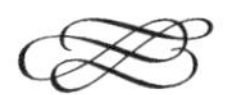

What kind of person was she? Feeling nauseated, she pressed a hand against her stomach, which was threatening to cause all sorts of embarrassing problems. Her body shook uncontrollably, but she refused to be sick in front of everyone.

Taking deep, calming breaths, she forced the cold air into her nose and let it out through a small hole between her lips. After a few minutes, the icy air did the trick, and her stomach settled. She could feel Paul's concerned stare, but couldn't meet his gaze. Not yet.

After the Rangers left, she let her horse follow Paul's as he led them back the way they'd come. Traveling in the protection of the ravine was a definite improvement from the day before. She didn't think she'd ever been this cold, and never wanted to be again. First chance she got, she was heading back to Texas. With Wade Phillips out of the way, she and the ranch were safe, her family avenged.

There were still problems. She needed her herd. What good was a ranch without cattle? Plus she needed to find where Phillips had put the deed to the Rancho, or his brother could take everything from her all over again.

The soft blue sky above should have cheered her up, but it did not. Instead, her body felt numb. She kept her gaze on her horse's ears, his neck drooping down as he plodded along behind the others.

Taken from one of the men killed while abducting her, the appaloosa's coat was white with light brown spots splattered over the hips. He was a beautiful horse. He was good-natured, and the only positive thing that had happened to her over the last few days since Phillips had killed her mare.

She didn't like the way Paul kept turning around and glancing at her. Since leaving the military post, Dean had asked several times if she was all right. She knew they worried about her. She worried about herself, too.

Feeling guilty was stupid, even though she had never killed a man before. Wade Phillips was a bad man. An evil man. He would have done the same to her without a thought. Still, it had been she who shot him.

They stopped for coffee, and Paul handed her several pieces of jerky, which she held in her lap. She drank the hot liquid, savoring the warmth of it seeping through her body.

He leaned against the chiseled dirt wall. "I'd like to tell you it gets easier—killing someone—but it doesn't. You had to do it," Paul said.

She stared into their small fire, the dancing flames calming her nerves. "To be truthful, I'm not sure what to think. I feel numb inside."

"That's normal."

For the first time since leaving the ravine, she met his gaze, her brows furrowed. "Did you kill many men during the war?"

He didn't look directly into the fire but stared at some point behind her. His lips thinned and nostrils flared. From the corner of her eye, she saw Dean lean forward as if he, too, was interested in the answer.

Paul took a deep breath. "Yes."

She waited for him to say more, but instead, he poked at the burning wood and added a few more twigs.

"Have you gotten over killing them?" she asked, hoping his answer would release her guilt. But, deep down, she knew it probably wouldn't.

His green gaze met hers from underneath his flat-crowned hat. "No, not really."

"That's what I thought you'd say." She let out a frustrated sigh. "I'll work through this like I've had to do everything else in my life." She added under her breath, "I just need a bit of time."

"Unfortunately, time isn't something we have a lot of at the moment."

"Excuse me?" She clenched her jaw, forcing down her growing annoyance at the man sitting across from her.

"Before we left, Colonel Davidson told me to be on the lookout for renegades. Two weeks ago, a hundred or so young Comanche warriors left Camp Wichita. Since then, there've been cattle and horses stolen from Flores' ranch, and his men were killed."

"And you still think this Flores person will be able to help us get the cattle back? Sounds like he's having his own problems with them."

He flung the last few drops of coffee from his cup into the fire then emptied the pot, dousing the spitting flames. Dean rewrapped the material around the jerky and repacked it with everything else in his bags.

Mounted, Paul stared down at her, his gaze hard. "We don't really have a choice. If you want the cattle..."

She played with the reins, twisting them around one hand and unwinding them, only to begin again. "I know you don't understand my decisions. Women don't run ranches. They stay in the kitchen. I've heard it all before, but I *want* the Sanchez Rancho—now mine since Phillips killed my stepfather. I know I can do it, woman or not! I need to sell off as many head as I can, then with the money, I can start rebuilding the herd in the spring."

Paul clenched his jaws then leaned forward against the horn. "Anna, I never said you couldn't or shouldn't run the ranch. You just seemed indecisive about what we're doin' out here."

She shook her head. "No. If Mr. Flores can help me get the cattle back from the Comanche, then we need to go talk to him."

He gave her a short nod then turned his horse around and continued along the gully bottom. Dean waited for her to get settled on her own mount, then fell in behind her.

Following Paul at a slow pace, her thoughts were muddled and confused. Wanting the Rancho and getting it was overwhelming—and a bit more than she'd bargained for. So many questions whirled around her mind, and before long she had a splitting headache. She needed her stepfather's guidance. He'd been a good father to her and Richard, raising them like his own children. She was going to miss him.

Her horse abruptly stopped, jerking her from her reverie. Dean moved around her and edged closer to Paul who stared at something on the ground. Suddenly, the appaloosa's head came up, ears twitching back and forth. He turned his head to the left, the whites of his eyes overtaking the light blue centers as he tried to see something behind them. Turning in the saddle, she glanced back. Several yards behind them, there was a narrow slit in the wall.

She slid off her horse and walked back to take a closer look. She pulled a few skeletal branches away from the black opening. A bush, long dead, hung from its roots and covered the crevice. She pushed it to one side, and found the dark hole larger than she thought. When she tried to get the appaloosa to go in, however, he shook his head and stepped to one side, pushing away from it.

Curious, she glanced down the path as the men disappeared behind a bend. She let the bush fall back over the wide crevice. On a small branch facing her, there was a smudge of red that could only be blood. Glancing around, she saw several more splotches along the dirt by her feet and another just inside the opening.

She climbed back up on the appaloosa and trotted after the men, noticing the farther from the opening they got, the more he calmed down. Her gut, along with the blood, told her something or someone close by was in trouble. She rubbed the side of the appaloosa's neck and murmured to him in a soft voice.

The men had moved even farther away, both of them trailing something on the ground. She glanced back at the narrow opening. She nudged his flanks with her heels. Startled, the horse jumped forward, trotting until they caught up to the men.

"Paul, there's something back there I think you should see."

Without looking up, he asked, "Were any of the men in Phillips' group injured?"

"No. Not until…" She took a calming breath. "Why?"

"There's a blood trail, maybe two."

"Paul."

He rose from his stooped position and turned around. "Did you see something?"

She nodded. "I found small splotches of blood by a narrow crevice in the wall. I think something, maybe someone, might be in there."

He frowned. "I didn't notice a crevice. Are you sure?"

She tamped down her mounting irritation. Why did men always question her as if she were empty-headed? "I'm sure. I pulled away the dead tree hanging over the entrance, obscuring it. There is an opening."

"There are quite a few places where the dirt has separated, making it look like a crevice."

She scowled at him. "Are you always this argumentative? I'm not stupid, and I know what I saw. It's a narrow path branching off toward the west, and it was hidden behind a dead tree. I wouldn't have even seen it if Burt here hadn't been skittish." She leaned forward and scratched the coarse hair behind his ears. "You did good, Burt."

Paul made a face, like he'd bitten into a sour pickle. "Burt?"

She shrugged. "I like naming my horses. He looks like a Burt."

Paul took a deep breath as Dean pinched his lips between his teeth, trying not to laugh. Shaking his head, Paul turned his horse and let her lead them back to whatever she thought she'd found. Climbing down, he handed the reins to Dean and pulled the dead bush away from the wall. Standing inside the opening, he listened for a few minutes. The hair on his neck rose, and he had the unsettling feeling he was being watched.

"You two stay here. I'll be back in a few minutes." Without waiting for an answer, he walked inside. He moved as fast as he dared, wishing he had his moccasins on instead of boots. Several feet in, he stopped and listened.

The light was dim and shadows clung to every surface, making it hard for him to see anything. The heavy scent of wet dirt filled his nose. There was enough room for maybe two people to walk shoulder to shoulder. Up ahead he could make out the outlines of either rocks or dirt piles that had fallen from the walls, partially burying the pathway. He was surprised to discover the path was wider than he first realized.

Somewhere close, he thought he heard a soft scratch, like cloth or denim scraping against rocks, but he couldn't be sure. He didn't like anything about this space. Part of him wanted nothing more than to turn around and head back, but he continued walking forward at a slow pace.

Behind him, one of the horses scuffed his hoof against the hard ground and a saddle creaked. As his eyes adjusted to the dim light, he pulled off the leather strap securing his gun and drew it from his side holster. Before he reached the first mound, a dark shadow separated from the wall and lunged, shoving him to the ground. He dropped his gun. Rolling over, he leapt to his feet, struggling to keep upright with the heavy weight draping over him, huge hands grabbing at him.

Working his arms between them, he shoved the man back. He didn't budge. The biceps now wrapped around him like a vice were the size of his own thighs.

The heel of Paul's boot skidded over loose scree, and they fell. The back of his head bounced off the dirt wall and scraped downward as they slid to the floor. Fingernails scratched the soft skin on either side of his neck. He twisted, reaching down to the stranger's waist with one hand, grabbing for anything he could use as a weapon. His fingers brushed over the edge of what felt like a knife, but he couldn't reach down far enough to pull it out of its anchor.

Whoever this was, he knew how to fight.

With his other arm, Paul worked until his forearm rested underneath the man's chin. He pushed up, forcing his head to lean back, but the man's hand lashed out and struck him in the Adam's apple. He coughed several times, feeling like the small bones were sticking through his windpipe.

"I don't want to hurt you..." he grunted, trying to clear his throat.

From somewhere behind them, a low voice said something in a language he didn't recognize, and the big man hesitated, his grip loosening, but the fingers remained wrapped around Paul's neck. The voice, quieter and weak, said the same words again.

This time, the man dropped his hands and rolled off. Lying on his back, Paul stared up at the sliver of blue sky peeking through the small opening above them.

"You soldier?" the hidden man said.

Paul propped himself up against the wall, unsure if he should answer or just get up and get the hell out of there. Leaving would be the smart thing to do, but no one had ever accused him of being smart.

He cleared his throat. "Not anymore. I fought in the War Between the States. Now, I'm just wanderin'." He saw Anna's pretty face in his mind. "Maybe I'll find me a home," he added in a low whisper.

He pulled in a deep breath. The scent of damp dirt sated his nostrils and calmed his tense muscles. He loved the smell of dirt, always had. He glanced toward the sound of the voice but couldn't see anything but several large boulders blocking the path up ahead.

"You from post? Know men who attack?"

Paul frowned. "You were attacked by soldiers? Were you rustlin' cattle?"

"No. We on hunt—trade horses for meat at ranch."

Whoever the man was, he was in a bad way as his voice faded. Paul crawled over to the man who attacked him and stared at the Indian's face. Eyes closed, he couldn't tell if the man was dead or alive. Taking a chance, he laid his hand on the man's chest and felt his heartbeat, steady and strong under his palm.

He pulled his hand away, sticky and wet, noticing the man's barreled chest was smeared with blood. He had several lacerations across his stomach and sides. Paul wiped his hand against his pants and noticed more injuries over the injured man's body. "Someone carved you up pretty good, didn't they?"

"Your friend's still alive but hurt," he hollered out to the man who'd spoken to him in broken English a moment ago, but his declaration was met with silence. Cursing under his breath, he walked forward a few feet, hoping he wasn't about to get himself killed, and found the second man lying on his back behind one of the large rocks, a patch of blood covered the left side of his chest with more blood oozing from a small hole above his left breast. His stomach was cut in several places, and Paul noted more blood on the man's leggings.

He knelt beside the man, feeling for the pulse in his neck, which wasn't as strong as the other Indian's, but he was still alive as well.

Hurrying back to Anna and Dean, he explained the situation, and Dean followed him into the passageway. It took some time, but they both managed to half carry, half drag the two men out and laid them side-by-side on the ground.

Staring at them, Dean frowned. "You said one spoke English?"

Paul nodded.

"But, sir, those are Indians. Comanche Indians. How in the hell are we supposed to heal them and stay alive afterward?"

Anna gave an unladylike grunt. "Then you know nothing about Comanches. They won't kill you if you save their lives. I lived on the Rancho for maybe three years before we were attacked. Several of the Indians were wounded. They, too, were Comanche. My stepfather took them in and healed their wounds. To this day, they are my friends. We trade with them. People need to look past the differences in skin and culture and see the good there too—on both sides."

Dean scowled at her. "Do you think I'm stupid? These are Quahadi Comanche." He pointed to the larger man. "And that is Quanah Parker, their leader."

CHAPTER 9

Anna stared at the two men, her gaze resting on the huge man. So this was the unstoppable Quanah Parker. She could see why everyone was intimidated by him. Even unconscious, he was intimidating.

She glanced at Paul then back down at Quanah. "What are we going to do with them? They are both injured, and we only have three horses."

"I'll go up top and gather some logs and tie them together as a makeshift travois." Dean mounted and gave them a crooked smile and pointed at Quanah. "Think he'll notice if his feet drag the ground? I'm not real sure I'll be able to find a tall enough-sized branch lying around to fit him. He makes you seem short, Paul." With a laugh, he left.

Paul gathered a few withered-looking plants, broke off several of the larger branches from the dead bush, and made a fire. With her help, they inspected the Indians' wounds. Both men had been shot and, between the two, she counted at least fifteen stab wounds. She glanced over at the smaller man. The bullet wound above his left breast, several inches from his heart, worried her.

From her saddlebag, she pulled out the extra shirt she'd brought with her, tearing the material into long strips while Paul cleaned out the worst of the wounds on both men. He bandaged them the best he could and wiped the blood and dirt from their other wounds. Now, all they could do was wait for Dean to return.

"Do you think they'll live?" she asked as Paul poured water from his spare canteen into the coffeepot then placed it on the fire to boil.

He shrugged. "Time will tell. I've seen worse."

"In the war?"

He poured their coffee and sat back against the wall, stretching out his long, lean form. "Yes." He stared at a spot beside her in the dirt. His only movement was the clenching of his jaw.

She blew on the hot liquid, relishing the fleeting puff of heat cascading over her face with each breath, and took a small drink, wishing she had a bit of milk to go with the sugar. Even sweetened, the strong bitter flavor was disgusting, but she drank it. Holding the tin cup between her palms, the warmth seeped into her frozen flesh while the hot liquid warmed her insides. "I understand if you don't want to talk about it. Several of our ranch hands fought—one for the Confederacy. It was a touchy subject for them too. Matter of fact, they would never answer my questions."

He swallowed the last drink of his coffee and poured himself another. "I still hear the volleys of gunfire in my mind. There was one soldier in our unit, couldn't have been more than seventeen. He took a shot to both legs and his pelvis, buck and ball, shattered the bones." Pain spread over his face and his eyes darkened, his brows dipping downward as he stared into the fire. "I've never heard screamin' like that. It never stopped. Not until he died. All I could do was hold his hand..."

"I'm sorry. I shouldn't have asked. No one should have to relive those memories."

He met her gaze and shook his head. "That's exactly what I should do. I have to remember why we fought the war. Every man has a right to freedom."

Taken aback at the anger in his voice, all she could do was stare. All the sorrow disappeared as he scowled at her, his gaze dark and fiery. He ran his fingers through his brown hair, which left it disheveled. She liked it better.

"Sorry."

She shook her head and finished her coffee. "Don't apologize. I feel as strongly as you do. No one has the right to own anyone else." She smiled at him. "I just don't bite people's heads off when voicing my opinions. Most of the time." She smiled when he pulled his collar up higher and lowered his head, refusing to meet her gaze.

"Sorry," he mumbled.

She puffed out a long breath of air between her lips. "Stop apologizing."

One of the men moaned. She held still, waiting to see if he would wake up. Even wounded as they were, they were dangerous men. She'd seen enough in her short life to know the viciousness of their attacks. Paul moved closer to the one Dean had called Quanah and laid the back of his hand across the man's forehead.

"He's burnin' up." He turned to the other man and felt his skin. With a worried frown, he glanced over at her. "They both are. We have to get them to the ranch soon."

She scooped some of the snow drifting down from the top of the ravine into her cup and held it over the fire, adding more so the water remained cold. Taking one of the leftover strips from her dress, she tore it into smaller pieces and dipped it into the water. Folding it in half, she laid it against his forehead. She repeated the motions until their foreheads and necks were covered, replacing or dipping them again as the heat from their skin warmed the cloths.

Paul handed her another cup of cold water and a piece of jerky. "Dean should be back any time. As soon we get 'em loaded, we'll head for Flores's ranch."

She wiped the blood and dirt from Quanah's forehead and replaced the older cloths with new ones. Finished, at least for the time being, she sat back and ripped off a small bite of the tough meat.

"What I wouldn't give for a thick, juicy steak with a side of new potatoes and Maria's soft tortillas dipped in honey butter." She missed the bossy cook who had always treated her like a granddaughter, cleaning her cuts and scrapes then wiping away the tears. Something her mother had never done.

"Who's Maria?"

"Our cook. She's dead too, isn't she." She held the jerky between her hands, which she clasped together in her lap. "I'm sorry for earlier. I had no right to argue with you. It's just..."

"I'm sorry." He glanced toward the bend in the arroyo. "You've had a tryin' time lately."

She stared down at her hands, searching for the right words to explain how she felt, which was almost impossible, because she didn't know herself. "My emotions are all over the place. I should be happy Phillips is dead, but...well, I've never killed a man before. Other times, because of the daunting task of finding my herd, I just feel hopeless. I don't like feeling this way. I've always been able to take care of myself." She gave a little shrug with one shoulder. "But now?"

"You'll get through this. Ma Floyd always said what doesn't kill us makes us stronger."

"I'm not really sure that helps much. She sounds like a strong woman—your mother."

"The strongest I've ever known. I never knew my real mother." He glanced down the empty ravine, wanting to change the subject and surprised he'd even mentioned his real mother. "We can't wait here much longer. The Comanches will wonder where their leader is and come a lookin' for him. Believe me, we don't want to be here when they arrive."

He repacked the saddlebags and walked along the sandy path to where it turned slightly to the west. With his arms crossed over his chest, he leaned against the hard-packed dirt wall and kept a lookout for Dean. The kid should've been back by now.

He didn't like their situation one bit; stuck in the ravine with two injured but very dangerous Comanches. Who attacked them? Dean also hadn't found out any new information about the missing soldiers he'd been sent to find.

He frowned, his thoughts returning to the sergeant he'd seen talking to Anna. The man's eyes were shifty, and his right hand never strayed far from his gun. More like a gunfighter than a soldier. There was something so familiar about him, but as of yet, he couldn't recall where he'd seen him before.

A dark shape appeared at the far end of the ravine. He made out Dean's lean-bodied form as he drew closer. He went back to the fire and stomped out the smoldering ashes. Scooping up a large handful of newly fallen snow, he dumped it on top and rechecked the Indians' wounds.

He didn't like the look of the chest wound. The skin surrounding the bloody hole was not quite as red as the blood, but it was close. The man was lucky, though. Two inches lower, and he would be dead.

"Dean's comin'. We need to get movin' before their friends come for these two. And they will come lookin'."

She stood, brushed off her riding skirt, and leaned a little, tilting her head to one side, trying to see Dean. "How much time do you think we have?"

"No tellin'. Depends on when they were attacked or what really happened. My guess would be a couple of hours, maybe a bit more if we're lucky."

Dean's horse pulled the travois into the small space. He swung his leg over and jumped down, brushing the snow off his pants and shoulders. "Had a hell of a…." Chagrined, he threw her a glance from underneath his wide-brimmed hat. "Sorry, ma'am. Had a heck of a time finding enough branches long enough and thick enough to support their weight. Went further north to get it down into the ravine without tearing the travois up."

"Anna, grab your blanket. Dean, hand me yours," Paul said as he grabbed his own from behind his saddle. She helped him spread two of them out as a cushion against the hard horizontal pieces of wood lashed together between the two long side poles.

As gently as they could, the men lifted Quanah to the travois first. Then they placed the other man beside him. She tucked the last blanket around them. Paul tied the men down using a couple of piggin' strings, careful to avoid their wounds. The English-speaking Comanche opened his eyes and glanced around, his gaze resting on Paul who leaned forward.

"We're takin' you to the Flores ranch. You'll be safe there."

The Indian stared a moment then nodded. "You know he is Quanah, yet still help?"

Paul smiled. "I help anyone who needs it."

"You good man. I, Redhawk. Flores good man too. He help Quahadis." His eyelids drooped but popped open again. "Quanah...live?"

"Yes. I'm more worried 'bout you though. You took a nasty bullet to the chest," Paul pointed to the place on his own chest. "Sleep, if you can." He waited for Redhawk's eyes to close again. When they did, he grabbed the reins and climbed into his saddle. Turning the roan's head in the same fluid motion, he took the lead, letting Anna stay in the rear to watch over the Comanches.

The ride through the ravine was uneventful until they reached the end. The wall there was much shorter as the ground rose, leaving a fall of loose scree and dirt about two feet high. He leaned on the pommel and stared at the short incline, which might as well have been ten feet high with the travois. Paul's gray roan sidestepped but gave Dean's black enough room to move several feet closer.

"Any ideas?" Paul asked, his gaze never leaving the slope of dirt.

"The travois won't fit through that, but the dirt seems loose enough. Maybe we can widen it a bit?"

Paul got down and dug his fingers into the frozen earth. They were in luck. The soil was hard chunks that broke apart without much effort and not the packed clay usually found here. He was able to knock down enough to make an opening wide enough for the travois. He tamped down the dirt slope with his boots so the horses wouldn't sink in and break a leg. He stepped back with a satisfied glance. "There. That oughta do it."

Grabbing the reins, he walked the roan up the slide without any difficulty. "Lead the horses up to lighten' the load. No need to take a chance." He pulled up his collar and shoved his hat down on his head to block some of the freezing wind and light snow beginning to fall again.

Glancing around, he could see farther now than earlier, a half-mile, possibly a bit more. The sleet had stopped, which would ease the difficulty of trying to find the ranch, he hoped. Not knowing the area, he couldn't make out Davidson's landmarks under the thick white blanket of snow.

He helped lead Dean's horse, skittish from the unfamiliar weight behind him. Anna followed without a problem. The three of them started out again, trudging a new trail through the pristine landscape as they worked their way toward the ranch.

CHAPTER 10

Paul smelled the wood smoke first, faint but there, and guided his horse toward the line of trees they'd been following for the last half hour. He turned in his saddle and met Dean's gaze. The kid nodded.

He glanced at Anna. "Smell the smoke?"

She lifted her face for a moment then scowled. "I don't smell anything."

"It's there." He faced forward with a small grin. The longer he was around Anna, the more he liked and admired her. Her beauty didn't hurt either.

He glanced up at the tall blackjack oaks standing among bur oaks and hickories. In the spring, the area would be breathtaking, and nothing like the grassland he was used to. Thick beneath the canopy, a large variety of shrubs grew, choking out the prevalent Indian grass covering the surrounding plains.

He held up his hand for Dean and Anna to stop while he scouted for a way through the trees. Not too far ahead, he found the opening. Going inside a few feet, he saw the wagon ruts. With a quick flip of his hand, he signaled to them and they followed as he led them down the path and underneath the skeletal arms of the canopy overhead. The scent of burning wood became stronger the farther in they went.

"I smell it now," Anna called from behind. Paul grinned.

Ten minutes later, they found the clearing. At the far end, butting up against the side of the mountain, stood a good-sized stone house. The dim winter light settled over the house and smaller building, both made from the same round orange stones. The barn sat tucked into the trees and lent a deceptive feeling of spaciousness to the small area. On the east side of the cabin, more behind than beside, he could see part of the corral fence with two horses peering over the top railing.

"Don't go no further, if you value your scalps!" a gruff voice hollered from inside. "Don't need no more visitors, so just turn around and go back from wherever you came from!"

Paul's smile widened and, in a well-practiced motion, he shoved his hat back on the crown of his head. "Is that the way you greet a friend? Never knew you to be so cantankerous, Cap!"

"Well, I'll be..."

The shotgun disappeared from the corner of the large window beside the front door, and a couple of thumps came from inside the house. The door swung open, and Ricardo Flores hobbled out on a thick tree branch whittled into a crutch.

"Gave me quite a fright! Never expected you to show up on my doorstep. Leastways, not here."

Paul dismounted and, with a hurried step, met the older man at the porch, which scaled the length of the home. Reaching out, he clasped his gnarled hand and gave it a hard shake.

Ricardo gave a loud belly laugh and pulled him into a bear hug. "It's good to see you, son. You're a sight for these sore and mighty tired eyes."

Paul stepped back and saw the pronounced lines showing on his friend's face. His eyes were red and bloodshot, as if he hadn't had a full night's sleep in a while. The last time he'd seen him, he'd carried a bit of extra weight around the middle. Now, he couldn't spare an ounce. "What's goin' on, Cap?"

He glanced around, noticing no one else had come out from the barn or house to greet them. Ricardo was close to sixty, and shouldn't be trying to handle even a small ranch on his own. Not smack dab in the middle of Comanche territory. It would be suicide. "Where're the others?"

Cap leaned a bit more on his crutch, his smile disappearing. "Dead. Hit pretty hard nigh two weeks ago. Been waitin' for Davidson to send help, but seems he has his own problems. Should've gone with them the first time they were here, but I guess I'm just too darn stubborn. Last raid, I took a bullet to the leg. I'm gettin' along better, but this ole body doesn't heal as fast as it used to."

He slid over a couple of steps and glanced behind Paul. "Well, now, seems like you folks ran into a bit of trouble yourselves."

"Nothing we couldn't handle." Paul motioned with his thumb to the travois. "Found these two in the ravine 'bout ten miles back."

Paul helped Ricardo off the porch, walking beside him to make sure his old friend didn't fall and injure himself more. Dean had already untied the two Comanches and was checking on their wounds when they stopped beside the travois.

Ricardo let out a small gasp and hobbled closer. Leaning

over, he asked in Comanche, "*Heights, hein ne-mah,* 'hello, what happened?'"

Quanah's eyes opened and a weak smile appeared. He raised his hand, grasping his forearm and responded, the older man leaning even closer to hear the softly spoken words.

Ricardo patted the back of the Comanche leader's hand and placed it over the blood-soaked bandages covering his chest.

He gave Paul a quick glance, his gaze quickly returning to the unconscious Indian. "Redhawk?"

Paul shook his head. "I'm worried. He's in a bad way. Bullet just missed his heart."

Anna stayed back out of the way while the men took care of the Indians. Her horse stomped at the hard-packed dirt, and the ranch owner glanced over his shoulder, noticing her for the first time. He started to say something to Paul, but stopped, his eyes narrowing in a frown as he stared. His lips moved as he muttered something under his breath, the words too soft for her to understand.

The ranch owner must have been quite handsome in his youth. His once black hair was peppered with gray, giving him a distinguished look. She narrowed her gaze and studied him, trying to find any similarities to her father. He was too thin, but she could still make out the strength he once had in the thickness of his arms. His upper lips was covered in a long-handled, thick mustache, more black than gray. She couldn't recall a single instance when her father's face hadn't been shaved. Even with the mustache, Ricardo Flores was still a handsome man.

She smiled and walked her horse forward. "Hello, Mr. Flores. My name is Anna Sanchez."

He limped forward a few steps. "Nice to meet you, ma'am.

You must be frozen on that horse. Don't have much to offer a lady, but the place is clean and warm."

Her smile widened. She liked him, the shy smile and his gruff voice. Similar to what she remembered of her father's, but not quite what she remembered. Eight years old was a long time to recall a voice, even one as dear as her father's "Thank you."

Paul moved to the head of the travois and crossed Quanah's arms over his chest. Gripping the corded shoulders, he and Dean carried him into the house, laying him on the blankets Ricardo threw on the floor in the small guest room.

They repeated the same careful procedure while moving Redhawk, placing him on the narrow bed. Paul unwrapped the blood-soaked bandages and gave a soft hiss. The chest wound was inflamed. The torn skin was hot to the touch and still seeping blood, although not as much as before.

The *tap, tap, tap* of Ricardo's crutch on the timbered floor sounded from behind as he moved toward the other side of the bed. He laid out clean cloths, silver forceps, a bottle of whiskey, and a small black bowl filled with a coarse black powder resembling gunpowder. Braced against his crutch, his chest heaved from the exertion.

"Not used to being up and around since I took that bullet. Been right lazy." He met Paul's worried frown with a slight smile and straightened a bit.

"Sit. I'll have Dean and Anna help. I don't want you as a patient, too." He opened the front door and hollered at Dean, who'd gone out to take care of their horses as soon as they'd deposited Redhawk on the bed.

Anna stood beside the large table. "If you tell me where the springhouse is, I'll get the water?"

Ricardo gave Paul a wink. "I'll help her gather up what we need. Not too old or crippled for that." He limped to the door and pointed to a small door at the back of the main living area. "Through there. Didn't want these old bones going back and forth through bad weather, so I built an inside access to the well. Rinse out the coffeepot sitting there by the fire. You can use that to get the water a boilin'."

He turned toward Dean as the young soldier stepped into the room and gave him a nod. "Good to meet you, young man. Name's Ricardo. Now, bring me the large metal bowl on the table if you don't mind."

Once the water came to a boil, Anna carried the heavy coffeepot with a dishrag wrapped around the handle and followed Dean into the bedroom. He placed the bowl on the small table beside the bed.

As she poured the boiling water into the bowl, she glanced at the bedframe. It was made from the trunks of several thin trees. It was beautiful, and much nicer than a regular metal frame. Throwing the rag on the floor, she set the almost empty pot on top.

She focused on Paul as he bent over Redhawk. Using the forceps, he dug around in Redhawk's chest with slow, meticulous movements. A few minutes passed, seeming more like an hour, then he pulled out the bullet. Picking up the whiskey bottle, he poured some into the wound and sprinkled a pinch of gunpowder over the wound. She handed him a needle and thread. His stitches, small and precise, impressed her. "You've done this before, haven't you?"

"A few times."

"During the war?"

He nodded. "And before."

"Paul was our company medic," Ricardo explained. "Not an official title, of course, but after the only boy who knew anything 'bout healin' was killed, Paul was all we had. Did right well, he did. Fixed me up quite a few times."

She stared at him a moment. Without saying a word, she

turned back to the task at hand. She rethreaded the needle and handed it back to Paul. With small, even stitches, he closed the front and back holes where a second bullet had gone through Redhawk's arm. She had to agree with Mr. Flores. His work was every bit as good as the doctor's back home.

They moved over to where Quanah lay. With so many stab wounds covering his body, as well as two bullet wounds, she couldn't believe the Quahadi leader was still alive. And then to fight Paul? He must be a sight to see in battle—a sight she didn't want to see.

When Paul was done sewing up the worst of the wounds, she folded up the extra bandage material and placed it on the floor beside the small table. Gathering up the bloody supplies, she walked back into the main room to wash them. She knew there would always be a next time, especially in Indian Territory.

PAUL STRETCHED, his muscles pinched from leaning over the bed for so long. Picking up the dishrag from under the pot, he dipped it into the bowl and wiped the blood from his hands.

The old man's dark-skinned wrinkles furrowed even deeper as he turned from the small window to face Paul. "What's that girl doin' all the way out here?" With an even more pronounced limp, he moved to the rocking chair in the far corner of the room and sat, holding the crutch between his bowed legs.

"She ran into some trouble back in Texas. Neighboring rancher decided he wanted both her and her stepfather's Rancho. With her mother's help, he almost succeeded."

Ricardo shook his head with a frown. "Her own mother?"

Paul nodded. "Rancher won't be comin' after her again. She killed him this mornin'."

"Hmmm. Good for her, though you need to watch her. Shock'll be setting in. Hard enough for a man to kill another man, but a woman?"

"She's tough, I'll give her that. Tougher'n any woman I've ever known."

"What's she doin' up here if her home's in Texas?"

Paul threw the bloody rag into the bowl and sat on the end of the bed so he wouldn't bother Redhawk. "Searchin' for the three thousand head of cattle Phillips stole from her stepfather's Rancho. That's actually why we're here. Davidson sent us to you, seein' how you're friendly with the Comanches an' all."

Ricardo smiled. "He did, did he? Well, he's got the right of it. I help 'em as much as I can. Trade them beef for hides and protection."

"Protection? They've not done much if you keep losin' cattle and horses."

"That's part of our plan," Ricardo said. "We're going to trap whoever's behind it. We know it's someone from Camp Wichita, but that's about it." He leaned forward, his crutch between his legs. "So, what can I do to help Miss Anna Sanchez?"

"We need to get the cattle back from the Comanches who stole them from the men who stole them from her."

"Only place to sell them out here is at Camp Wichita. Or me. Why didn't her stepfather come with her? Not right sendin' a pretty young thing like her up here alone to do a man's job."

Paul gave him a crooked smile. "Stepfather's dead. Anna thinks she can run the Rancho by herself."

CHAPTER 11

Camp Wichita, Indian Territory

Sergeant John Taylor walked across the military compound, not paying any particular attention to anyone or anything as he made his way toward one of the outlying buildings. This meeting with John Hardin wasn't supposed to happen until tomorrow. He'd hired the Texas gunslinger to lead a small group of renegades to hunt down the damned Comanches who'd stolen the cattle from Miss Sanchez. With Hardin here now, something had gone wrong with their plans.

He glanced around to make sure no one was near the half-constructed stone building to see him enter. The last thing he needed was for one of the soldiers assigned to the construction task to question him. Not too many things got past those damned buffalo soldiers.

His eyes adjusted to the dim light as he entered through the large open doorway. Glancing around, he could make out the building's partitions for the separate rooms, and there was one plastered wall opposite where the fireplace would be.

The tall, thin figure of John Hardin walked through the back door. He looked exactly as a hired gun would be expected to look. His eyes took in everything, missed nothing. His black, knee-length greatcoat hung open, snow still resting on the shoulders. Inside the coat, the special holsters sewn into his vest were visible, as were the two guns ready to be drawn.

"Don't have all day, Taylor."

Hardin's low gravelly voice made the hairs along the back of John's neck rise. The man standing before him was one of the most ruthless killers he'd ever known. And, thanks to his father, he knew many outlaws. Hardin had been credited with killing at least twenty men, but there were probably more.

"You called this meeting. What happened? Did you get that murderin' savage?"

The gunslinger nodded and crossed his arms, a move Taylor had seen him do several times before drawing. "Quanah and Redhawk took several bullets, and a couple of the boys enjoyed cutting them up a bit. Problem arose when a group of men interrupted."

Taylor lit a cigar, chewing on one end as he tried to control his anger. The last thing he needed was to get shot before he carried out his plans. A year, maybe two, and he would be a rich man. With his father's connections along the outlaw trail, he'd managed to rustle enough cattle and horses to set him and his father up nicely. Now all he had to do was run old man Flores off his ranch.

"So are they dead or not?"

Hardin's face remained closed, his dark eyes hooded. Taylor couldn't gauge what thoughts were in the other man's head, so he refrained from saying anything until the gunslinger answered the question.

"Left them bleeding out in a ravine. The hands are dead too."

"Then why insist on meeting this morning? What's so damned important that you'd risk everything I've set up?" Taylor started to take a step forward, then thought better of it when Hardin's left hand moved closer to his gun.

"Flores is still alive and has help. Two men and a woman rode to his ranch with what Dougherty thought was a month or two worth of supplies. He wasn't close enough to tell though…just saw a travois trailing behind them with a load."

Taylor tossed the cigar butt to the ground and began pacing. "Damnation!" he muttered, then stopped and turned on his boot heel to face Hardin again. "I want you to dry gulch Paul Daniels. The other's just a boy—wet behind the ears. He shouldn't be trouble, but if he is, kill him too. The girl's spirited. I want her."

"What about Flores?" Hardin asked.

One side of his mouth curled up in a sneer. "Several days ago, Rangers brought in a couple of prisoners. Lucky for me, one of 'em talked. Girl killed his boss, a man named Phillips. Davidson sent a wire to Phillips's brother who's on his way here. I want the Flores' ranch and the girl—and he's going to help me get them."

He walked through the door but stopped, glancing back at Hardin, who still hadn't moved. "Give me a week, then meet me at the north mountain where we met before. You'll get your money…only after I have the ranch and Flores is dead."

Hardin stared after Taylor, watching him walk across the snow-covered grounds to the stately headquarters building. He'd seen the small group Taylor had mentioned as they left the military post a few days before and was familiar with the man leading them. Did Taylor know who he was dealing with?

Lieutenant Daniels and his unit had fought against a battalion of Confederates during the last days of the war. For a white man, he'd moved like a cat stalking its prey, and had killed more men in thirty minutes than he himself had in an hour of fighting. The way Daniels moved reminded him of Indians.

He stared down at the dirt floor, then walked back through the building to where his horse was tied. Mounting, he turned toward the north mountain, knowing this was going to be a long week.

CHAPTER 12

Two days had passed since their arrival at the ranch. Though the Indians were healing, Redhawk's chest wound wasn't mending as hoped.

Anna stared out the small window. The house, smaller than the one in Texas, was cozy. The surrounding land was beautiful, even covered in a winter blanket. She liked it here.

"How're the patients doing today?" Ricardo hobbled into the small room, leaning heavily on his crutch, and stopped beside the bed.

"The same, really. Why isn't Redhawk's chest wound healing?"

"Well, it was more serious than the others, so I'd expect it to take a bit longer to heal."

"I suppose."

"Would you like some company?"

She smiled and nodded. "I miss my books."

"As you can see from my small collection in the other room, I also love reading. When I moved from Louisiana, I think I was more worried about my books than anything else."

"Oh, I thought Paul said you were from Missouri."

"I am, but lived longer in Louisiana. So as soon as my military term was up, I moved here. Not an easy place, but no bad memories." He hobbled around to the chair, sitting beside the bed since she was already occupying the rocking chair.

She smiled. "I understand about that. My mother moved my brother and me from New Orleans all over the state. Until she married her fourth husband in Texas, we'd never known what it was like to feel settled anywhere."

Ricardo stared at her until she felt very uncomfortable under his intense gaze. "Mr. Flores, is something wrong?"

"May I ask how old you are?" he said, his voice more husky than normal.

She frowned. "I'm twenty-five years old."

His scowl deepened. "Was your brother younger or older than you?"

"He was two years younger."

He dropped his face into his palms, scrubbing his whisker-covered cheeks with his gnarled hands. "After all these years…" He raised his head, his gaze watery, and gave her a tremulous smile. "You look so much like Josephine, only prettier. Just before you all disappeared, she'd turned so bitter and resentful."

She dropped back against the chair, the worn joints creaking, as his words sunk in. "What are you saying, Mr. Flores?"

He wiped the few tears dotting his wrinkled cheeks with a tattered handkerchief and sighed. "My father remarried and moved us to Missouri for a better future when I was about fourteen. He died shortly after arriving, and when my stepmother died, I joined the army. I was stationed in Louisiana in '46. Your mother and I met at a governor's ball.

For me, it was love at first sight. She was so beautiful, her smile stopped my heart.

"By the time your brother was born, there were rumblings of war throughout the country. The day after you turned eight, I received a missive to report to my commanding officer. Upon my return home, I discovered my family gone. I searched for your mother, you, and little Ricky until the war broke out."

She stared at the man in front of her, wide-eyed and lips trembling. His story explained so many things—her mother dragging them from bed and leaving New Orleans in the middle of the night, telling them their father was dead, why she'd never seen her father again.

She covered her trembling mouth as the significance of what he'd told her sunk in. With tears in her eyes, she walked across the room and threw her arms around him. "My mother hated the nickname Ricky—now I know why," she whispered against his neck.

Redhawk moaned. Reluctantly, she pulled away from her father's embrace to place her hand on Redhawk's forehead. His fever had broken in the early morning hours, but he wasn't out of the woods yet. Trying to stop the infection from growing worse, Paul had reopened the chest wound the previous evening, which was something new for her. Cleaning and suturing she'd done before, but the healing afterward wasn't something she'd ever dealt with. The cowhands would just take care of it themselves, which was fine by her.

Pouring a tiny amount of Mr. Flores's—her father's—whiskey into the wound seemed to help as well, so she'd begun refilling the small hole once every two hours or so throughout the early morning hours. Glancing beneath the bandage, she let out her held breath.

"It looks better. See how the skin has faded to a light pink?" her father asked.

"It's not as hot to the touch now, either." She met his twinkling gaze. Her heart swelled, filling her chest with so much happiness. The moment was surreal, incredible. She'd always hoped but never imagined she'd see him again; now she was in his house, watching over his injured friends, and they were together.

Did this change her plans for her stepfather's Rancho in Texas? She didn't know, but for the moment, she was content to remain here for a while. The Rancho wasn't going anywhere.

With a quick tap of his crutch against the floor, Ricardo rose. "Now, our meal won't cook itself. I'll see what I can round up for us to eat."

She sat down in the rocking chair and stared out of the room's one modest-sized window, her emotions raw. Too many things had happened to her in such a short amount of time, and she was so overwhelmed. Her life had changed so drastically in such a short time. Her mother no longer ruled her life, and the man who'd taught her so much about life was dead. Just when she began to accept what had just happened to her, something else came along. Good or bad, it didn't matter anymore. She was emotionally exhausted.

There was another problem. She hadn't said anything to Paul earlier, but without the deed her mother had given Phillips, getting the cattle back wasn't the only thing that would save the Rancho.

Outside, the snow-covered trees marked the gentle slope of the small mountain as it converged with the valley. Still-visible footprints led away from the house and down what seemed to be a narrow trail. Paul had explained yesterday that a smaller barn had been built away from the main corral so rustlers couldn't steal all the horses.

How like the man she remembered—always thinking ahead, planning on things to come. Too bad she hadn't inherited that trait. Maybe she could have avoided everything that had happened.

She watched a little white rabbit hop out into one of the boot tracks, wiggle his nose, then continue hoping through the dense brush. No, she decided. If she had prevented losing her stepfather or the ranch—even killing Phillips—she would have never found her father again.

Or Paul. She would never have met him. She rubbed the ache above her left breast.

"You...sad?"

The voice was scratchy and hoarse because of being unused. She turned away from the beauty outside, meeting Redhawk's brown gaze. His eyes were almost black in the room's dim light. She gave him a lopsided smile. "Not really. I was just admiring the land. It's beautiful here." She took a deep breath and crossed her arms over her chest. "That's not quite true. With everything that has happened to me, I feel a bit…lost." She sighed and shook her head. "It's confusing."

His eyes closed a moment, and he moved his right arm up and laid his palm on top of the bandage with a small wince. He opened his eyes again and met her gaze. He didn't need to voice the question. She knew the information he wanted. If she were in his position, she would want to know, too.

"You will be fine and back to your great warrior self, but not as fast as you would like." She poured him a cup of water and, with one arm underneath his head, helped him drink. "Your wound was bad."

"You fix?"

She sat back down in the rocking chair. "No. The man who found you—Paul Daniels—fixed you and your friend."

His eyes widened and for the first time, glanced to the

other side of the room where Quanah slept peacefully. "Quanah is no-heet-s hasta, *well*?"

She nodded. "He was up a bit this morning, but he mostly sleeps. Like you."

Redhawk grunted.

"You speak English well. Who taught you?"

"My father friend of white shaman. Father believe understanding key to our people living together with white man."

"Your father is smart." She frowned. "I didn't think the Comanche wanted to get along with the white people?"

"Father not Comanche. He Kiowa. Father learned much from Thomas Smith—he trade with Kiowa."

She glanced at the still sleeping Quanah. "Does he speak English too?"

He shook his head with a grin. "He knows few words. Quanah no like Whites."

"I know a little about what happened to his mother. Is it because of her?"

"She love Peta Nocona. He love her—die soon after soldiers take her away."

She turned back to Quanah. His light gray eyes were open and staring at her. A tiny frisson of fear crawled along her arms, but she ignored it and smiled. "You feel better?"

Redhawk translated for her and Quanah gave a curt nod. Seeing no malice or anger in his eyes calmed her nerves even more. "Would you like something to eat? There's still some leftover stew from last night's supper. It was really quite tasty."

She glanced back at Redhawk. "I'm sure you're hungry too. The stew is good. There are also Mexican tortillas if you like?"

His eyes widened and a small grin appeared. "With honey?"

She smiled. "Yes, with honey."

"Reecardo make good tortillas. We come often for those. He always give us more for children." He struggled to sit up on the bed. Without a second thought, she helped him then straightened the sheet over his lap and propped a pillow behind his back for comfort.

Wishing she understood their language, she listened while Redhawk translated their words. Quanah's large body relaxed, and his face transformed when one corner of his mouth rose in a small grin. He liked the tortillas too.

She ran her palms over her riding skirt, smoothing out the wrinkles from several day's wear. "I'll go get your food." Leaving the door open, she heard the men's low voices as they talked back and forth.

Anna and Paul carried food-laden plates into the room, and the Indians stopped talking. She placed her tray on Redhawk's lap and straightened. "Do you need help eating?"

Redhawk shook his head and picked up a warm tortilla, dipping it in the small bowl of honey.

His expression of wonder as he chewed made her smile. "Don't forget the stew." She turned around as Paul stepped back from giving Quanah his food.

"I did not go into the ravine to hunt you—I didn't know you were there. I would like for us to be friends," Paul said.

With his mouth full of meat, Quanah mumbled, stuffing in another spoonful before he finished chewing the first bite.

"He says you good fighter. Would like to fight again when healed. Soldiers need to answer for crimes. He allow you to fight for them."

Paul's brows drew together in a dark scowl. "I want to find those soldiers myself. Before we left Wichita, Colonel Davidson told me he had units out looking for you, but their orders weren't to fight your tribe, only to convince you to return." He thought a moment then asked, "Redhawk, have you seen these soldiers before?"

He nodded. "From Camp Wichita. Four soldiers ride with Cheyenne and Arapaho. My people go there. Wild Horse is Kiowa chief. He too old to control young warriors. They want to fight, prove skills. He hoped soldiers help, but he wrong. Many left—I join with Quahadis."

"Could you describe them, these soldiers?"

He nodded. "One is sergeant." He swiped three fingers across his upper arm. "I see markings on sleeve. Has face of *sciate*—what you call weasel. Others dirty and stink like buffalo skinners."

"Hide men," Paul confirmed. "Disgusting, if you can even call them men."

Redhawk said something to Quanah in Comanche who grunted a response. Redhawk smiled. "Your words please him. That is good. We do not want you as our enemy, Paul Daniels. We have enough enemies. The Quahadis need friends."

Paul nodded. "I would be honored to be your friend—and friend to all Quahadis. I don't agree with what the military and white government are doing to the tribes. There is enough land in the territory for everyone."

Anna stood beside Paul, listening to their conversation with growing admiration. His quiet manner and strength impressed her. She wasn't sure when it happened, but she now understood her way of handling things might not always be the best way. Jumping into situations before she really understood them wasn't smart. And she wanted to be smarter about doing things.

She studied Paul from the corner of her eyes. He needed a shave, but the beard stubble didn't detract. If anything, it made him more handsome and rugged. Forcing her eyes down to her hands, which were clasped in front of her, her face warmed. She'd known many handsome men, but these feelings were unfamiliar to her. He made her feel dainty and petite.

After cleaning up in the kitchen, she wiped her wet hands on the dishrag and laid it on the counter to dry. Turning, she pushed her shoulders back with determination and walked toward her father's room. She raised her fist to knock but hesitated.

There was so much she wanted to talk about, but still, she didn't quite know what to say to him. Pulling in a deep breath, she held it and knocked on the rough wood, hoping she wasn't disturbing him. Behind the closed door, the clumping of his crutch grew louder. She let out the pent-up air with a soft sigh.

Her father pulled open the door and stood there, his salt and pepper hair sticking up. Her mouth twitched. His sleepy eyes and dazed expression confirmed he'd been asleep.

"Anna? Is something wrong?" His brown gaze swept the room behind her then settled back on her face.

"May we talk?"

He opened his door wider for her to walk through, closing it with a soft *snick*. He waited until she was seated in the room's one chair before he sat on the end of his bed, holding his crutch between his legs.

Now that she was here, she wanted to leave again. She didn't know what to say. Instead, she clasped her hands in her lap and stared at the floor. After several minutes, she gathered her courage and, in a rush, asked him the questions running through her mind. "Tell me about yourself, your family. What happened between my mother and you? Why you left us?"

He raised one eyebrow, his mouth twisting to one side. "That's a few questions. You would like to know more about where you come from, eh? I was born in southern Texas in a small border town. My father was a Comanchero and traded with the Comanches. He fell in love with a beautiful Comanche girl and married her. My mother died when I was born, but I honored her heritage."

Anna felt her heart miss a beat. "So…that means I'm part Comanche?"

He nodded with a smile. "As I said earlier, my father remarried, but his new wife didn't like Texas and wanted to return to her home in Missouri. Never got on too well with her. She never could stomach my Indian blood."

"Why didn't you come home? Mother told us you were dead…"

He turned the crutch around several times, twisting it in a circle between his palms. "I am sorry she did that. I loved—love—you and your brother more than you'll ever know. You haven't yet told me how Ricky fares. He's old enough now to have his own family."

She shook her head. "I'm sorry, Papa, but Richard never came home from the war."

He nodded and cleared his throat a couple of times. "Lots of young men never returned home." He glanced at her with a sad gaze. "He fought for the Confederacy?"

"No. Neither he nor I agreed with slavery. No one should be owned by another. He wore his Union Blue with pride. I know he was a good soldier. You would've been so proud of him."

"I am, Chiquita. I am. You haven't mentioned your mother. How is she?"

She shrugged, the familiar pet name bringing back long-forgotten but pleasant memories of childhood, her father chasing after her and her brother, their taking turns riding on his broad shoulders. "I really don't know. Phillips told me she had returned to New Orleans to marry a plantation owner.

"Not that I care, especially after she all but sold me to

Phillips. I don't remember a single moment when she was happy, even a tiny bit. She could never have enough possessions and always schemed for more. She was a very unhappy person. Paul never saw her body at the Rancho, so I assume she really did go back to Louisiana." She didn't like the way her father's shoulders drooped. "Papa?"

"I'm sorry for everything you've had to endure, Chiquita. If I could fix it all, I would."

She smiled. "I know. It's what Jonathan Sanchez would've done too. He tried to be a good father, although it didn't come naturally for him. He taught me a lot—how to brand cattle, how to ride, even how to manage a ranch."

She didn't want to admit, even to herself, that her dream of running her stepfather's Rancho might be over, especially now that she knew she was part Indian. She would be an outcast in the white society.

No one would have to know.

With her luck, though, someone would eventually find out and she'd lose everything. The problems surrounding her were overwhelming. The pressure weighed on her shoulders and heavy in her mind. Maybe she should just give up the Rancho and stay here with her father…

He stood, startling her out of her reverie, and pulled her into his embrace, holding her tight against his thin chest. "I'm sorry. For all you've been through, I'm so sorry."

Her father smelled like pine trees. She remembered his scent, and had missed the way it enveloped her when he'd hugged her. "I never stopped hoping Mother was wrong, and that you really weren't dead. I missed you, Papa."

"I missed you, too, Chiquita. I missed you, too."

She pressed her cheek against his chest and let her long-stored tears flow. After thinking her father was dead, she'd found him again. This time, she wasn't going to let him go.

CHAPTER 13

Paul stared incredulously as Dean grabbed the last two biscuits and buttered them. He'd already eaten four. "Where do you put it all?" He'd never seen anyone eat as much as the kid did.

Dean shrugged but instead of answering, he took another bite. Quickly swallowing, he changed the subject. "Been seven days since we found the Comanches. Think they'll be leaving soon?" He scooped up the gravy coating his plate with his last biscuit. "You are a fine cook, Miss Anna. I will miss meals like this when I'm at Camp Supply. Won't have tasty desserts either." He gave her a toothy grin. "Did you bake a pie?"

"You know I did. Found the last of Papa's canned apples, so I made an apple pie just for you." She placed a generous piece on each of their plates. The last two pieces she took to Redhawk and Quanah, who still hadn't left the bedroom.

Sitting on the bench beside her father, she took a bite and set her fork on the plate. "What do you make of their story, Paul? Why would four soldiers lead a small group of Arapahos and Cheyennes out here?"

"Rustlin'," he answered and finished the last bite of his pie, wiping his mouth with the back of his hand before gulping down the hot, black coffee. Perfect ending for the perfect meal. But that was only his opinion. Truth be told, as long as he had coffee, he'd be fine.

"This ranch is the only one in this area. Easy target to take both cattle and horses. Aren't enough men here to stop it."

He glanced over the table at Ricardo, who was scraping the last bit of thick piecrust around the plate with his fork. "Cap, how many head have you lost?"

Ricardo met his gaze and shrugged. "Not sure. Boys up and left me after the third raid, but they didn't make it far. Found their bodies and buried them in the valley back of here. I reckon I've lost seven hundred, maybe eight." He shrugged again. "Your guess is as good as mine anymore."

"Horses?" Dean asked.

"Thirty, maybe a few more."

"Papa, how many times have they been here?"

"The last time they hit," he slapped his injured leg, "was when this happened. That was the fourth time. They never attacked the house. Mostly, they stole the animals at night while we slept." He shook his head and shoved the plate away. "Not much more to take."

Anna glanced around the table in bewilderment. "What's gotten into you three? So we fight. Nothing new there. We can always ask the army to help out. Colonel Davidson seems to know what he's doing. Why can't they send a unit out to patrol?"

Paul shook his head. "We will fight, Anna. That isn't the issue. The military is stretched too thin for the area as it is. Like Texas, there are too many miles of open territory for such a small force to patrol. With the government moving all the tribes to reservations, there aren't enough men to stay on top of it. Indians fight. They battle each other, the military, and the settlers who are taking away the only life they've known for thousands of years."

A small frown furrowed her brows. "What about the Rangers?"

The hint of a smirk curled one side of Paul's mouth. "I'm afraid there are problems enough in Texas to keep them there. Besides, they only come into Indian Territory to chase outlaws or renegades from Texas. I'm afraid we're on our own up here."

Scowling at him, she turned to her father. "Would the Comanches help? Papa, you said you were on friendly terms with them—like family." She gave him a pointed stare. "You feed them, and they watch out for you. Why wouldn't they help, especially after we saved the life of their chief?"

Ricardo shook his head. "I can't say. The Quahadis have enough trouble taking care of their own selves." He tilted his head toward Paul. "Like he said, they're fighting for their lives, just as we are. Quanah is a very intelligent man, and, yes, he is like a brother. He knows I help his people as much as I can, but asking him to stop and help save my ranch is out of the question. The best we can hope for is to find out who is behind this and why. Might be, even Quanah's people will get a reprieve if we do."

Paul drummed his fingers against the table's rough wood. "The Comanche raid south of here—in Texas and Mexico?"

"Normally," Ricardo answered.

He glanced over at Dean then met Ricardo's dark gaze. "Who do you think's behind the raids here? This isn't their territory."

The old man nodded. "Been askin' myself that same question."

The guest room door opened without a sound. Only the slight shuffle of moccasins against the floorboards announced the warriors as they entered the room. Quanah spoke first to Redhawk who translated.

"We owe you a debt for all you have done for us." Redhawk said, glancing at Quanah as he continued speaking. "Comanche honorable people. I give my word. We will help fight against those who try to cheat our friends."

Quanah's light gray eyes stared into Redhawk's for a moment. When the other man nodded and motioned with a quick tip of his head, Quanah turned to Ricardo and cleared his throat. "You my brother. I help."

Ricardo nodded.

Paul stared at the Indian but kept his features from revealing his surprise at the Indian's well-spoken English words. "Thank you, Quanah. You are indeed a great leader. An honorable Comanche."

For the first time since arriving at the ranch, Quanah's chest puffed out a bit more, and his stern face relaxed as he and Redhawk went back into their room, closing the door behind them.

Anna smiled and opened her mouth, but before she could say anything, Paul's hand went up, cutting her off. He listened for a moment then rose, walking to the front window and glancing outside. Without turning, he moved toward the door. "Soldiers. Ricardo, tell Redhawk and Quanah to stay quiet and keep away from the window until I can get rid of them."

"But if they can help..." Anna pleaded.

He turned, giving her a hard gaze. "These men are not here to help." Without another word, he opened the door and walked outside, warily approaching Sergeant Taylor who, instead of sitting erect like a soldier, slouched on his horse. Paul's eyes narrowed as he tried to place the man before him, again without success.

"So, Mr. Daniels, you and your party made it."

Paul heard the soft treads behind him and knew Anna had followed him onto the porch.

Taylor sat up straighter and smiled. "Good day, Miss Sanchez," Taylor said. "I'm glad to find you safe and well. This area isn't the best to travel in with the Quahadis raiding."

Anna stepped off the porch, and Paul wasn't surprised when she stopped beside him, smiling up at the sergeant. "Thank you so much for your concern, Sergeant Taylor."

"What brings you here, Taylor?" Even to his own ears, Paul's voice sounded abrasive and curt.

"I was sent by the colonel to ensure your safety and make sure you found the ranch without difficulty. He also wanted you to know about that thievin' Comanche, Quanah. He and a few of his men were seen not too far from here. Probably trying for the cattle and horses again."

The entire time he talked, the sergeant's gaze moved from them to where the upper corral fence was nestled near the back of the house.

"Oh, but—"

"Sorry to disappoint, Taylor, but we haven't seen anythin' unusual since our arrival. Been right quiet if you ask me—if the reports about a Comanche uprisin' are to be believed. Other than the Rangers stoppin' by, it's been mighty peaceful."

For the second time, Paul had interrupted Anna. She thought the sergeant cut a fine figure as a soldier, but gut instinct told him this man wasn't being truthful. There was something off about him, and until he figured out what it was, the less contact she had with him the better.

Taylor's sharp gaze snapped back to meet his. "The Rangers were here? Why?"

"Bout three, maybe four days ago now. Takin' a couple of

injured prisoners to Wichita. Surprised you didn't run across their trail."

Taylor's eyes narrowed into slits, but other than that, along with only the slightest hardening of his features, he showed no outward emotion. He glanced at Anna and, with a sharp tug against the brim of his dark blue hat, gave her a nod. "Good day, ma'am." He turned his horse's head but hesitated. "You all better keep an eye open. Those Comanches are renegades. They'd kill you just as soon as look at you."

Paul's gaze followed the soldiers as they went back through the trees along the narrow path. The other two men never spoke but kept glancing over the area as if looking for something in particular. He also didn't like the way they stared at Anna, who picked that moment to hit him on the shoulder.

"What do you mean by interrupting me again? And you were quite hostile to Sergeant Taylor...who, by the way, never did anything to you."

Dean stepped off the porch as she stomped into the house. "You certainly know how to treat a woman, I'll give you that. Handling her well, if you ask me."

"Oh, shut up," Paul muttered. "I'm not concerned with makin' her feel good, just keepin' her safe and alive," he lied, not liking Anna's interest in Taylor at all. He was irritated with himself for letting it bother him in the first place. He'd agreed to keep her safe, which he'd done above and beyond, in his opinion. But anything more...

He turned his attention back to Taylor and glanced back toward the tree-lined path, frowning. "I can't put my finger on it, but somethin's off with him."

"Noticed it too." Ricardo limped up to them and leaned against his crutch. "He's got shifty eyes. Don't trust people who don't look me in the eye."

Paul shook his head. "That's not it, although I agree. I know him from somewhere, just can't place him."

He followed Paul's gaze as he stared at the trees where the soldiers disappeared. "What did you say his name was?"

"Sergeant Taylor. John Taylor."

Ricardo let out a soft whistle. "Boy, when you make enemies… There was a John Taylor back during the war. Wastrel and scoundrel, as I recall. After that last battle in Louisiana, he was one of the men you reported for desertion during the main skirmish. Taylor must be a fancy talker to have only been sent to Indian Territory and not shot after what he'd done. Shootin' prisoners of war is a hangin' offense."

Paul continued to stare down the empty path then shrugged. "That must be it. Had to report quite a few bounty jumpers in '64. Don't remember as many close to the end though." He walked back to the house with Ricardo and Dean right behind him. "Still, there's something about him…"

Anna met them at the door, worry etched into her pretty face. "They're gone!" She twisted the small towel between her fists. "Quanah and Redhawk—they're gone!"

TWO MORNINGS LATER, Anna was the first one up. After washing up as best she could, she boiled the water for coffee. Knowing she still had a few minutes to herself before starting breakfast, she poured herself a cup and walked outside. The morning was clear; the sky was a beautiful azure blue, and there wasn't a cloud in sight. Unlike her mind, which was still filled with indecision about what she should do…continue to try to find her cattle, or stay here with her father?

Her gaze followed the trail of steam as it rose over the hot liquid, the wisp of vapor curling upward. A sudden movement near the tree line caught her attention. A small deer stuck its head out from between two trees and looked around. She held still as the animal put one leg out then another until it stood in the yard, its muzzle turned up, sniffing the air. He took another step and froze, suddenly darting back into the copse.

She smiled. Her father had chosen well. This area was beautiful. Her home in Texas had a solitary desert beauty about it. But it was lonely. Here, the surrounding trees enveloped her like a warm blanket.

She turned to sit down on the porch chair and found what resembled a folded up fur rug in the seat. Setting her half-empty cup on the porch, she carefully unfolded the soft brown fur to find several more folded pieces of even softer leather inside.

She picked up the creamy yellow deerskin on top of the small pile. Shaking it one time, she found herself holding a long-sleeve shirt with small bits of metal, beads, and tufts of animal hair sewn into the fringe hanging from the chest vee and shoulders. There were two more men's shirts like the first, but it was the white deerskin leather underneath that drew her eye.

With a soft touch, she ran her fingertips over the intricate geometric beadwork decorating the front yoke and along the tops of the arms then splitting apart at the neck. The colorful patterns were exquisite, with beaded fringe just below the chest design and more fringe around the waist and hem.

She raised the dress and pressed it to her front, holding it against her waist. She couldn't help but admire the painstaking care someone took to create something so beautiful. She was on the short side, so the dress fell to her ankles, but the arm length was perfect.

She glanced around the snow-covered yard, then back down to the dress, a small smile playing over her lips. When she noticed the pair of fur-lined buffalo hide boots nestled inside the dark blanket, she laughed. The brown fur of the boots blended with the robe. What magnificent gifts!

Gathering everything up, she ran into the house. Her sudden appearance startled the three men, who looked at her wide-eyed. "Look what our new friends left for us!" She laid the shirts on the table between them and showed them her dress and boots. "Aren't they beautiful? I've never seen the like!"

Paul pulled out a shirt from the pile. With a grin of his own, he glanced over at Ricardo who held his up against him. "Quanah is a generous man. Wonder if he treats all his friends this well?"

Ricardo nodded. "He owes you his life, which he doesn't take lightly. Neither does he trust easy. You and Dean earned his respect by the way you helped them. Something he didn't expect from white men. These gifts are his way of telling us he's judged us as honorable men."

CHAPTER 14

Anna stood by the fireplace, watching her father's slow movements as he gathered the things he would need for the round up. They discussed his leaving earlier, but she still didn't like it. He wasn't healed enough to gather up whatever cattle had been left by the rustlers.

"Papa, please don't go yet. Waiting a few more days won't hurt anything. The cattle and horses will still be there. Surely, nobody would think to rustle anything when there's two feet of snow on the ground?"

"You know better, Anna. Those thieves will take every last animal I got if they can, and it won't take a little snow or bad weather to stop 'em either. No, I have to get out there to see what's left of my stock."

She folded her arms across her chest and rubbed one hand up and down the soft deerskin sleeve as her worry grew. "What about the herd the Comanches took from Phillips's men? They belong to me now. There's close to three thousand head. Can't we try to get them back first?"

"Those cows are long gone. Indians take the cattle and horses then resell what they don't want to ranchers or other military units who aren't aware they've been stolen. Quanah told me himself. He'd steal cattle from one fort then sell them at another. Lucrative to say the least, and in their minds, a fair trade for the loss of their lands."

"But, it isn't right to do that—it's stealing!"

"You're thinking by white standards, daughter, not Indian. Everything you see out there was their land, for hunting and living. Now, here we are. Did we pay the Indians for the land we live on? I did, but most do not."

She thought about what he'd said while he finished packing the food and ammunition in his saddlebags. All she'd ever known were the rights and wrongs of a white moral code. Her father was right. She had been close-minded in her way of thinking, and didn't like it.

Despite standing in front of the blazing fire, a cold chill rode up her body as he pulled his Winchester off the wall. He also grabbed two pistols.

With reservation, she picked up the pistols and followed him out the front door toward the barn where Dean waited, sitting atop his own horse. The black pawed at the ground with his hoof, tired of waiting.

Ricardo checked the saddle, then placed his saddlebags behind it and piggin'-tied his bedroll. He shoved the rifle into the bucket and took one of the pistols from Anna and tucked it in the front waistband of his pants. The other he dropped into his coat pocket for easy reach. He stood in front of her for only a second before pulling her into his embrace.

"We've a lot of missed time to make up for, Chiquita. I'll be back soon."

"Just be safe, Papa," she whispered into his chest. "I love you."

"I love you, too. Now, you take care of Paul while I'm gone. He's a good man and needs a bit of soft in his life. Go easy on him with your high-spirited personality. He didn't want to stay behind, but I need to know you're safe."

"Not sure whether you mean that as a compliment or an insult."

"I'd have you no other way. It's your bright spirit that keeps an old man like me a comin' and a goin'!"

"Will you be okay out there with just Dean?"

"Sure I will. Dean's a good kid. Still wet behind the ears, but he'll learn. He won't be the first man I've taught how to round up cattle." He climbed into the stirrup and turned his horse's head, following Dean as they headed for the grassland on the other side of the mountain.

Standing there until her legs were numb from cold, the only sounds she heard were the chirps and calls of several birds in the skeletal tops of the nearby trees. When her fingers turned to chunks of ice, she turned and walked back into the house, wondering where Paul had gone.

She cleaned up what little mess there was from breakfast and poured herself a fresh cup of coffee, the milky sweet scent soothing away some of the apprehension she'd felt about her father leaving.

The loud stomping of his boots on the porch was her only warning before the door latch lifted, and Paul stepped inside. Setting the half-empty cup on the small squared table beside her, she walked over to the fire and poured him a cup. Taking it in between his palms, his long fingers laced together through the handle as he blew on the hot liquid.

After a few sips, he moved to the table and sat across from her. "Thank you. Bitter out there. No wind would be better, but I've learned that in this territory, wind is always a blowin'."

She topped off her own coffee and refilled the pot to brew more. "How long have you been here?"

"Came here with my sister in '56 then joined the war in '63, so off 'n on about twelve years."

She frowned. "I thought only the Indians lived here."

"Mostly. Grew up in Colorado and took a wagon train east with my sister...adopted sister, actually. Found her a husband in the Cherokee Outlet, so we stayed."

"Do you get to see her often?"

"No. I was on my way to their house for Christmas when we stumbled on your predicament. Megan knows better than to expect me, so if won't matter none if I'm a little late."

She sat a moment in stunned silence. "Christmas is only a couple of days away! How could I have forgotten?"

One side of his mouth turned up. "Well, reckon' you've been kinda busy—losin' your cattle and bein' kidnapped twice and all."

"Nice to see I've amused you a little."

"More'n a little, I'd say."

Paul walked to the counter and wiped out his cup, laying it upside down beside the others. "Think I'll go see if I can get me a deer or two for dinner and a bit of jerky."

"That sounds good," Anna agreed. "I'll bake this afternoon, biscuits and bread."

He hesitated in front of the closed door, his hand on the latch. "Might be late getting back, so don't worry if I'm not back by supper." He opened the door and quickly stepped outside, closing it behind him.

She scowled at the door. He'd been acting different toward her since her father left, standoffish. She couldn't figure out why, and it bothered her. With a sigh, she got up and placed her cup beside Paul's, staring at the two cups. She liked him and his quiet manner. The way he thought before answering her questions. His good looks didn't hurt either, but she had no idea what he thought about her. Did he think of her as a simply a friend, or a burden?

Preparing the heavy cast iron skillet, she mixed up the biscuit dough and patted the batter into the pan and placed the score lines. While the biscuits were cooking, she went into the springhouse and grabbed the jar of cherries she remembered seeing. Wanting to do something special to thank Paul for everything he'd done for her, she baked him a cherry cobbler for dessert.

She was pulling the bread from the oven when she heard Paul knocking the snow from his boots on the porch. He entered the house, holding a bound deer hide. He untied the skin and laid out several huge chunks of red deer meat.

"That should hold the two of us until your pa and Dean return. I figured on getting some jerky out of it, so you take what you want first."

She pulled out the two chunks of meat and cut one of them into four pieces, leaving the other for Paul to jerky. She placed two of her pieces in a large stoneware pot, covering them with sour milk to preserve the meat, and placed it in the cool springhouse. With the last two pieces, she rubbed a mixture of herbs and milk into the cuts of meat, rolled them up, and tied them with twine.

Aware of Paul's watchful gaze, she tried to ignore him while she browned the meat in a bit of beef fat. Once browned, she put the pieces in a crock of water. She added two more logs to the fire then placed the crock in the fireplace.

From the corner of her eye, she kept stealing quick glances at him. He'd shaved, which made his face look younger and so handsome. He'd also combed his shaggy brown hair, but the ends still curled over his collar.

"Never seen it prepared like that." He continued to slice the deer meat into long strips for drying into jerky.

"One of my favorite things to do growing up was sit in

the kitchen with Maria. My mother hated it, of course, but at least I learned how to cook."

"Have you and your ma ever seen eye to eye?"

"She isn't the easiest person to get along with. She thought children shouldn't be seen or heard. And there was only one way for a proper lady to act—her way. Unfortunately for her, I was never proper. She meant well, I think, but there was never any common ground between us.

"Growing up, my best friend was a black mare Papa gave me for my sixth birthday. Mother was horrified. Not because of the horse, but because of the split skirt and saddle. I would be riding like a man. Needless to say, I didn't get to ride a lot." She let out a snicker at the memory of her mother's shocked expression.

How was she going to manage if she went back to Texas? She might be able to keep her father's family a secret, but there was always someone who asked questions. She hoped her father would ask her to stay here, making her decision easier.

PAUL WAS a bit surprised when Anna remained silent during most of the meal, although it suited him just fine. Talking had never been his strong point with women. Normally, he opened his mouth, said the wrong thing, and the lady never spoke to him again.

He liked being alone, and until recently, he'd never really thought about settling down with a wife and kids. Thanks to the Floyds, he knew what a real family was, but he had too many unanswered questions about his own past. Like why his parents left him like they did. A part of him didn't really want to know why, but sometimes he couldn't help but wonder.

He shoved the thoughts back into the part of him he kept

locked away. Thinking about his past was a waste. Nothing could change what had happened.

Although since meeting Anna, he found himself wondering more often than not what having his own family would be like. Hearing the giggles and squeals of his children, seeing their brown hair and eyes. He liked Anna's eyes, dark and expressive...but tonight they held sadness, which bothered him. He didn't like seeing her upset, but didn't know what to say to help.

Sitting back and resting his clasped hands over his stomach, he groaned. "I haven't eaten that much in a coon's age. You took those cookin' lessons to heart. Ma Floyd's cobbler never tasted near that good."

She blushed, and the pink hue covering her cheeks was becoming, erasing the sadness. She'd done something different with her hair, too. Instead of the thick braid wrapped in a tight knot on the back of her head, it now hung loose, the long black strands waving across her shoulders. She was beautiful.

He wondered what it would feel like to run his fingers through her hair. His gaze moved down to her full lips, which glistened in the lamplight when she ran the tip of her tongue over them.

Alarmed at where his thoughts had turned, he stood, shoving his chair back with a loud *squeak* as the legs ground against the floorboards. Picking up his plate, he reached for hers and grabbed her hand instead. Their eyes met. His heart fluttered, and his insides turned all quivery.

"Sorry 'bout that." He released his grip as she handed him the plate.

Together they cleaned up. He added a couple of logs to the fire, and in the quiet of the evening, they sat in silence on the sofa drinking their coffee. Outside, the soft calls of a bird sounded then went silent.

"Tell me about your family. What are they like?"

He shrugged. "Don't rightly know 'em."

She frowned. "I thought you said you grew up in Colorado?"

"Don't talk about it much." In truth, he never talked about it. He took a gulp of the hot liquid. "I was raised in Colorado by a family who found me abandoned on the trail headin' through Kansas when I was about five years old or so. Don't know who my real parents are."

She placed one hand on his arm and squeezed. "I'm so sorry, Paul. I know how that feels."

She pulled her hand away, and he immediately missed the feel of it against his skin. "Had a good life with the Floyds. Taught me right from wrong and loved me the same as their own sons. Not complainin'."

"Still..." She sighed. "Dean and Papa will be okay, won't they?" She fidgeted and the leather seat popped underneath her. "I mean, Papa's not completely healed. I don't believe he should be on a horse looking for cattle. It's too soon."

"Your pa's a strong man—strongest man I've ever known. Stubborn too, but not too thick headed to know when he needs to rest. Dean's a good kid. He'll watch out for him."

"I know." She sighed, staring into the fire then down at the empty cup in her lap. "I grew up thinking he was dead. Now that I have him back again, I'm terrified something bad will happen." One tear slipped down her cheek, which she brushed away, but another one soon followed.

He groaned inwardly. One thing he couldn't stomach was a woman's tears. Made him feel guilty when he hadn't done anything. Taking her cup, he set it beside his on the floor and pulled her into his embrace, tucking her small body next to his. She was a perfect fit.

She sobbed into his shoulder, her hands fisting around the soft leather of his shirt. All he could do was hold her and hope she stopped soon. Whenever his sister cried, he'd always made her laugh, ending the spell. But with Anna, he wasn't sure how, so he let her keep crying.

She stopped with a soft hiccup and released his shirt, smoothing the soft leather with her fingers. The repetitive motion drove him insane. He closed his eyes and tried to think of anything but the feeling of her hand on his chest, but nothing helped. With a bent finger under her chin, he raised her face. Staring into her shiny brown eyes, he leaned closer and brushed his lips over hers.

Before he wanted to, he pulled away, waiting for his much-deserved slap. Nothing happened.

He opened his eyes to her brilliant smile. "Do you always kiss a woman to get her to stop crying?"

His mouth rose in a jaunty grin. "No ma'am. Not regularly anyway."

She smacked his chest with a loud 'ohhh' then burrowed closer, pulling his arm back around her shoulders. "You are still a very strange man."

"Yes, but I think you like strange."

"Hmmm, I think you might be right." She turned in his arms and stared at him. "I've never been with a man before...like this."

He held her cheek in the palm of his hand, the skin soft as a downy chick. "I would never do anything to make you feel uncomfortable, Anna."

Her gaze, more gold than brown in the flickering red-orange light, met his. A small smile played over her lips. "I'm comfortable right now," she whispered.

He pulled her to him again, his lips gentle at first then more forceful as he deepened the kiss. She kissed him back with a small sigh. Curling up against him, he wrapped his arm around her shoulders and pulled her close. He forced his eyes open several times as he tried to stay awake, knowing the last thing he needed was to compromise Anna. He held her tighter so that not even a breath of air could get through their bodies.

Only tonight, though, would he allow himself to enjoy the feeling of her body against his. As soon as this was all settled, he would be leaving for Colorado. His future didn't include Anna or settling in Indian Territory.

The fire died down to red embers, and neither one noticed when the other fell asleep.

CHAPTER 15

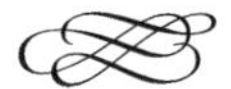

Two miles south of the ranch, a horse and rider struggled up the end of the ravine. Taylor had been waiting for the man to arrive, but didn't think he'd be stupid enough to travel alone through Indian country. Only a man on a mission, or running from something—or someone—would choose to ride through Comanche and Kiowa territory by himself. Not even winter stopped the savages from taking scalps.

As he drew closer, the rider suddenly noticed them and paused. Taylor's gaze narrowed. From the report his man had given him the day before, the man who was going to kill Flores was close. From the hard set of the stranger's mouth and the desperation driving him here, he thought he knew who this man was, but he needed to be certain.

"Long way from home?" Taylor called out.

The man didn't answer right away, waiting until he drew up in front of him and Hardin. His eyes shifted from left to right then back to him. "Are you from Camp Wichita?" He still hadn't answered Taylor's question.

"We are. You're takin' quite a chance travelin' through Injun country. This is Quahadi territory."

"Don't care about Indians. I'm looking for someone who came up this way awhile back. A woman. Maybe you've seen her? Her name's Anna Sanchez. Got word from a Colonel Davidson that my brother, Wade, had been killed."

Taylor met Hardin's dark gaze then turned back to the stranger. The report he'd received from Williams about Wade Phillips' brother had been correct. Keeping his voice flat, he replied, "She and two men." Taylor pulled back on the reins as his horse lowered his head several times and side-stepped, wanting to run instead of standing still. "Why do you want her?"

"She killed my brother."

"So you're lookin' for revenge?"

"I'm goin' to make her pay for what she's done!"

Taylor smiled a not so nice smile. "Davidson was mistaken. What if I told you it was her father who killed your brother? Maybe we could work something out—you kill the father and leave the girl for me?"

The man frowned. "Didn't expect to hear a soldier say something like that."

Taylor's sneer grew. "I'm not a regular soldier."

The man relaxed. "I'm listening."

CHAPTER 16

Ricardo mopped his brow with his shirtsleeve, more from habit than anything else, and shoved his well-worn wide-brimmed hat down over his head. It had been two days of hard work, but they'd managed to gather almost four hundred head and were getting ready to move them closer to the house.

He glanced at the far end of the small valley at Dean, wondering about his background. He was a good worker and respectful with his 'yes, sirs' and 'no, sirs'. Didn't know much about cattle, but he asked questions, listened when Ricardo told him to do something, and caught on fast. He smiled and gave the kid a quick salute as he rode beside the last twenty steers.

His horse turned to make its way over to the makeshift pen area when he heard his name. Jerking his head around, he saw Dean standing in his saddle, pointing.

"Behind you!" Dean screamed.

Ricardo raised the Winchester from across his lap and was in mid-turn when a sharp tug pulled down his arm. Two more tugs jerked him from the saddle. He landed on his back, staring at the white puffs floating across the bright blue sky. The day was beginning to warm up, but he only felt the cold as it seeped through his body. There wasn't much pain, but he knew he should be hurtin' pretty bad from those bullets.

He thought about Anna, her lovely face hovered over him. He smiled and tried to raise his hand to touch her cheek but could only lie there. From a distance came the sound of gunfire from both sides of the valley.

He'd had a good life. Not as long as he would've liked, but, nonetheless, a good life. Several more shots, followed by a high-pitched scream.

He hoped the kid made it…

John Taylor's gaze followed Dean as he rode away hunched down on his horse, large clumps of snow and mud flying them from the horse's hooves. The lieutenant got off a lucky shot, hitting Dougherty in the neck. Now he was down to three men. Didn't matter. Layout of the ranch didn't need many men, but several more soldiers he'd bribed to help him were on the way once those renegade Indians showed up.

He'd only visited the ranch that one time, but he figured he saw all he needed to. With the house backed up against the mountain, those inside couldn't sneak out the back, nor could they get to water. Holed up, they wouldn't last long.

"Let's go, boys. We have a house to take, and people to kill."

MORNING HAD dawned several hours before when Anna opened her eyes. She held herself still, staring into the fire-place. The logs had burned down to small pieces scattered on top of a pile of gray ash. She closed her eyes and took a deep breath, letting it out slowly. Her head was resting against Paul's warm chest and the steady *thump, thump* of his heartbeat beneath her cheek was comforting, yet frightening at the same time.

What have I done?

So as not to wake him up, she grasped his wrist and carefully moved it down until his hand brushed the sofa. Lifting her head, she eased away from him and stood. Rocking her feet from heel to toe, she stepped away. On the third step, she heard the rustle of cloth against the leather seat cushion behind her.

"Goin' somewhere?"

She sighed and turned around. Her face felt hot, and she knew she was beet red. "To get the fire going. It's a bit chilly in here."

"Let me do that. You get the coffee started. Tastes better when you make it."

She frowned as Paul pulled on his boots. When had he taken them off? She glanced down at her own stocking feet and couldn't remember taking her boots off either. He piled several thick logs on one arm, balancing it against his broad chest, then he stacked them on the ashes. Before he caught her looking at him, she grabbed the pot and went to fill it with water.

After the coffee had boiled, she added a spoonful of sugar and a spot of milk to her coffee, her thoughts returning to the previous night's kiss. Kisses. She poured the black liquid into a second cup and carried it over to where he knelt beside the fire. She sat back down on the sofa and sipped her drink, enjoying the heat from the fire as it seeped into the room's chilled air.

Thankful the warm blush covering her cheeks wouldn't be noticed, she was horrified with herself. She was so disappointed with herself and her actions. Paul had never said he loved her, much less liked her. Yet at the first chance, she'd practically slept with him!

But then she remembered how wonderful it felt to be wrapped up in his arms. She had felt safe, much safer than she'd felt in a long time. And the way he'd kissed her. She traced her lower lip with her finger, her heartbeat speeding up as she recalled his kisses.

She glanced at his handsome profile, dumbfounded. She suddenly knew why she'd been so hesitant to make a decision about returning to Texas. Paul wouldn't be there with her. Sometime during the last two weeks, she had fallen in love with this man.

"Your father should be back by nightfall. Cap didn't figure to find many—" The sound of muted gunfire interrupted him. He set his coffee on the floor and charged from the room without looking at her.

She pulled on her fur-lined boots then grabbed the buffalo robe she'd hung on a peg by the door. Throwing it around her shoulders, she raced out after him. Inside the barn, he had his roan bridled and was almost through cinching up the saddle when they heard Dean's weak yells.

Paul ran from the barn, meeting Dean in the middle of the yard as he slid from his horse and into Paul's arms. His shoulder and arm were covered in blood. Glancing behind him, she held her breath, waiting for her father to arrive. Dean said something, but she didn't understand. She couldn't understand. Slowly, she moved toward the path.

"Anna!" Paul yelled, running toward her as the muffled sounds of several horses reached their ears. He grabbed her and jerked her toward the house, Dean following close behind.

He pushed her inside and barred the door behind Dean. "Anna. I need you to take care of Dean's wound." He raced toward an old trunk half-hidden in the corner of the room and pulled the lid open. Inside, she could see boxes of ammunition and several pistols. He took them out, making sure they were loaded, and laid them on an empty shelf at the bottom of the small bookcase on the wall adjoining her father's bedroom.

"Where...where is my father?" she stuttered, still standing beside the table.

Paul glanced over at her and frowned, not liking the paleness of her face. Her eyes were too wide, and she looked like she was about to faint. "Anna, help Dean!"

The shout seemed to pull her from her stupor, and she raced into the guest room where she'd left the supplies used to treat Quanah and Redhawk. Setting them on the table in front of Dean, she pulled open his shirt. She cleaned the bullet hole in his shoulder and sewed him up.

"You were lucky it didn't break anything. It made a clean exit."

She couldn't look at him. Instead, she concentrated on wrapping the wound with a bandage, yet allowing him full range of motion of his arm should he need it.

"Anna…"

She met his watery gaze with her own. His chin trembled a moment then stopped as he pinched his lips together in a straight line. She shook her head and began cleaning up the small mess, putting everything back in the basket, and walked through the springhouse door.

Paul refilled his rifle, placing cartridges into the empty spots on his belt while Dean pulled three more rifles down from where they hung on the wall and loaded them. Taking out two more boxes of ammo, Paul threw one to Dean.

"Go to the guest room. It's not ideal, but the window should allow you to see if someone tries to come in on that side of the house." Paul said, watching as Dean tucked the ammunition underneath his arm. Holding the box against his side, he picked up a second rifle then marched out of the living room.

"Hey, there are hidden holes in the wall! I can look through the top one and the hole beneath it is large enough for the end of my rifle."

Paul glanced around the outer room, wondering if his friend had placed more holes around the house. He noticed two knots, one on top of the other in the kitchen and another set by the fireplace.

"There's holes like that in here too!" Anna yelled from her father's room.

Paul heard rather than saw her come back into the room, her steps clipped. "Take the trunk into the well room and gather up all the food you can and some blankets. Worst case, we'll have to make our stand in there. Might save our lives. Cap was smart."

WITHOUT A WORD, Anna did what he said and gathered the items, taking them to the springhouse in several trips.

"I need you to man the hole in Cap's room. Dean's in the other room, and I'll manage these."

She frowned. "There are two sets of holes in here. How are you going to shoot through each of them? You are only one person."

Paul walked toward her but stopped as she stepped away. The color had returned to her face, but her brown eyes were haunted, her eyes swollen from crying. "We'll get through this, Anna. I promise."

A hint of anger seeped into the depths of her eyes, replacing the anguish. "Don't make promises you can't keep." She turned on her heels and marched into her father's bedroom. He couldn't help but admire her strength. She was a strong woman. A woman to ride alongside a man, not behind him.

"Paul Daniels!"

He turned back to the window, peering around the edge of one sill. Outside, mounted on cavalry horses, were Sergeant Taylor and three other men. One was a dark, thin man wearing a long coat with crossed gun holsters over his chest. The others were soldiers, but he'd never seen them before.

His gaze returned to the thin man. His movements were few, and he sat his horse like an expert with no emotion on his face. He wished he were closer so he could see the man's eyes. He could judge a man by the look in his eyes.

"Daniels, you might as well give up now. You're not goin' anywhere!"

"Think I'll stay right where I am. Kind of like it here—all warm and cozy. Fire is blazin' somethin' fierce. I'd invite you boys in, but you don't seem quite friendly enough." It might be the last thing he did, but they were going to pay for killing Cap, especially John Taylor.

A distant memory from many years ago hovered in the back of his mind, and with it came the coppery scent of blood and the sound of tears. He narrowed his eyes as he stared at the sergeant's anger-filled face. His eyes had become mere slits, and the way the lower part of his face looked swollen…

Paul shook his head, careful to keep back from the window. All it would take was one careless moment. The other two men were restless, their horses stomping and shaking their heads as they picked up on their riders' moods.

"Come on, Taylor. Let's take 'em now. Cain't go nowheres but through the front door."

"Shut up, Biggs. You'll wait cuz I tell you to wait."

The other man's thin voice spoke louder than Biggs'. "Where's the money, boss? You promised us money."

With one hand holding his reins, Taylor swung his other arm through the air in front of him. "This is money. With the cattle, we don't have to set a stake for anything now that the old man's dead. Soon, we'll have it all."

"What do you want, Taylor?" Paul hollered.

"Your death, you miserable cur! You're nothing but dirt under my boots and always have been—a dirty Injun is all you are!"

Paul squatted under the window, staring at the crevice between the wall and the floor. Always have been? Other than the war, when had he known him? He stood back up and peered out front again. Two of them were gone. Only Taylor and the stranger remained.

"Look sharp! Anna, go across to the fireplace. If anyone goes around to your side of the house, Dean will get him first," he whispered in a loud hiss so the men outside wouldn't hear him.

"We've met before?" Paul hollered back, wanting Taylor's focus to remain on him and the front of the house. "Think I would've remembered someone like you. Must not have made a good impression."

He knew the insult wouldn't sit well, and even from inside the house, he heard the man's mumbled threats. He remembered Taylor from the war, after Cap reminded him of course. Who could forget a cold-blooded killer like that?

He also recognized the thin, dangerous man sitting just behind Taylor. Everybody in the surrounding states had heard of John Wesley Hardin. So this was the famous Texas gunslinger? Paul couldn't help but wonder what stake he had in all this. Cap would never have had dealings with him, much less any other gunslinger. Cap was one to uphold the law, no matter what.

"I have a little payback for you, Daniels!"

"You struck those men down in cold blood, Taylor. They were prisoners, unarmed and wounded. You deserved to be hanged, not sent here!"

"I was demoted because of you!" Taylor raised his pistol and fired in quick succession, five bullets smashing into the stone house, one shattering the window.

Paul cussed, remembering he hadn't locked the shutters, and ducked as a thousand shards cut into him, slicing his face and hands as he tried to cover his body. Grabbing up the rifle, he shoved the barrel back through the hole and fired. Taylor's horse reared back, throwing him to the ground, and bolted toward the path through the trees.

The heavy acrid scent of gunpowder filled the rooms as more shots sounded from inside and out.

"Got one!" Dean yelled and, with his box of ammo and guns, ran to the hole in Ricardo's room. "Paul, we have a problem. There's Indians out there too. Counted at least three on this side of the house."

"Two more on the north side. Paul, what if they're with Quanah and Redhawk?" Anna asked.

"They'd never come from behind us—we wouldn't be expecting them, so they'd stay up high, shooting from above. But neither of them are healed enough to fight, and unless some of their men are close, they wouldn't have had enough time to get to their camp," Paul said.

"Oh, well okay then," Anna added and fired, her body shoved back from the force of the shot. "Now there's only one on this side."

Paul shook his head at her rather strange humor. If that's what it was.

Anna glanced over at Paul. Not only was she heartbroken about her father, but she was also scared. She didn't see how they were going to get out of this unscathed. There were still two men and at least four more Indians. A volley of gunfire interrupted her thoughts as she stared through the small space between the barrel of her Winchester and the mortar between the rocks. She fired back as Taylor continued to scream.

"Your mother was nothin' but a squaw! Pa killed her man and forced her to work for him. She was nothing more than our slave! It was you who got her killed! Never could do what you were told and Pa got sick to death of you. He was done with her anyway, so he beat her to death and left you by the side of the trail! No one would miss either one of you!"

She saw the pain etched on Paul's face. Her heart ached for him and what he'd lost. What they had both lost. She started toward him but stopped when he glanced at her with such anger. "Stay where you are. It's what he wants, for us to forget what we're doin'. Just go back to your post."

A door closed in her mind. Her apathy dissipated like steam, and she walked with determination back to her seat and picked up the rifle. She stared through the hole and forced her gaze to not wander back to the aggravating man who'd worked his way into her heart.

CHAPTER 17

It was after dawn, and they'd been inside the house since the afternoon before. She leaned against the heated fireplace rocks and closed her eyes. Thanks to the men outside, sleeping had been out of the question. As she'd fallen asleep, one of them would fire into the house, waking her up again. That had gone on all night, but for some reason, they had stopped about an hour ago.

Had they given up?

What a ridiculous thought. Why would they fight so long, then disappear? Instinctively, she knew the men's absence didn't bode well for their situation.

Her gaze followed Paul as he walked past her and into the well room, as he called the springhouse. He was probably checking the remaining ammunition. They were down to only five boxes, which he'd counted not thirty minutes before. If the men came back and picked up where they left off this morning, those five boxes weren't going to last long.

"I'm going to go check on the horses," Paul muttered as he walked to the front door. Pulling it ajar, he waited for gunshots. When nothing happened, he eased the door open a bit more and glanced outside.

"Paul?"

He shook his head. "They're gone or hidin'. Probably hopin' we let down our guard." He gave her a quick grin. "If you hear gunshots, you'll know they're still out there."

"This is no time for jokes," she muttered as he snuck through the front door. Glancing into the adjoining room, she found Dean asleep on her father's bed. She sighed. At least one of them was going to be rested when the men came back. And they would come back. This she was sure of. Taylor was greedy. He wanted what her father had built, but she wasn't going to let him take it without a darn good fight!

She couldn't help but think about her father's body lying in the same spot where he'd died. To lose him so soon after finding him again was almost unbearable. Her heart felt like a hunk of stone, weighing her down.

Did fighting for her father's home mean she was willing to stay here? She still didn't know what she really wanted. Getting up, she stretched and walked to the window, peeking underneath the quilt, keeping out as much of the cold winter air as possible since the glass was gone. Nothing moved. She let her gaze rest on the barn. From its dark center came the soft nicker of one of the horses.

Paul threw the bucket of oats into the trough, uncaring that the force of his throw sent some of the kernels cascading over the side and onto the tamped earth floor. He shook his head and met his horse's light blue gaze.

He scrubbed his fingers through his already tousled hair and shoved his hat back on his head. "We're in a mess of trouble with no clue how to get out of it. Cap's dead, and we're runnin' short on ammo." He paced in front of his horse, who stood chomping on the grain.

Somehow, he was going to have to think of a way out of this situation, but his mind kept going back to waking up with Anna yesterday morning, her body curled up against his, the sweet smell of her hair in his nostrils, and her soft skin.

With a low moan, he turned and leaned against the short wooden partition between the stalls. Wrapping his arm around the post, he glanced over at the appaloosa, a slight smile curling one side of his mouth. "Burt," he whispered. "Who names a horse?" He knew the answer. Someone with a huge heart. Someone like Anna, that's who. He sighed. "What am I supposed to do now?"

ANNA WALKED across the room and peeked through the doorway of her father's room. Creeping inside as quietly as she could so as not to wake Dean, she picked up the quilt lying on the rocking chair and gently laid it over his long legs.

Walking back toward the fireplace, she hesitated. She didn't want to sit. As jittery as her insides were, she needed to be moving around, and didn't want to stay inside a moment longer. The fact that the killers were still out there seemed miniscule to her frantic drive to escape.

On a whim, she went to the springhouse. Dropping the bucket into the well, she lowered it until she heard the slap of wood hitting water. She pulled it from the well, balancing it on top of the wall, and grabbed the dipper tied to the handle. Scooping out the ice-cold water, she took a long drink.

The small room was dark and dank, the sharp scent of wet earth permeating her nose. On the far side wall hung a shelf, still full of canned food her father had painstakingly prepared. A pressure built inside her head, and the room grew smaller.

She leaned against the rough rocks surrounding the well and stared at the wall facing her. To get her mind off her father and not curl up on the floor and cry, she thought about Paul and what he'd told her about his family. How could someone be so cruel to a child?

She groaned. "What must he think of me, moaning and complaining about my life when his was so much worse? At least I knew I was loved."

She stared at the rocks covering the dirt wall. What she wanted more than anything right now was her father. At the thought of all the wasted time and their stolen future, a sharp pain tore through her chest, and her eyes filled with tears. She turned to leave, but from the corner of her eye, she saw something odd that she hadn't noticed before.

She hastily wiped her eyes with the backs of her hands and picked up the bedding thrown over the rusty ammunition trunk. Dropping the small pile on the ground, she pushed the trunk out of the way and stepped back.

The wall was lined with flat slate rocks. When she first saw them, she assumed it was for support so the dirt wouldn't cave in. Now, she wasn't so certain. In the middle of the wall stood a taller piece, its top sharply angled above the others. She frowned. Why would her father have done that?

She pressed against the rock. Nothing happened. With all her one hundred twenty pounds, she pushed again and was quickly rewarded with a small click. She let go and the piece of slate swung toward her like a door. Opening it all the way, she found herself looking into a dark tunnel.

She grabbed a lantern from the mantel and lit the wick. Before she could talk herself out of it, she went inside.

Thankful she wasn't scared of tight, enclosed places, she pushed away the curtain of tree and plant roots hanging from the ceiling above her. Gradually, it narrowed until she could no longer walk upright and had to lean forward, almost bent in half. A few more feet and she had to crawl.

Abruptly, the tunnel widened into a small grotto placed between a fall of boulders. Crawling out, she breathed in the cold air and stood, stretching the muscles in her back and wishing she'd grabbed her warm buffalo robe.

She examined the inside of the cave. There was enough space here for three or four people, if they were small. This place had definitely been used before. In the center was a pile of dry wood. Starting the fire, she walked to the entrance and peered out, keeping herself as hidden as possible. The last thing she needed was for Taylor or one of his men to see her here.

Surrounding the hole in the rocks was a thick bush and several oak trees. They stood close enough together so that only a thin dusting of snow managed to fall behind them. With one arm wrapped around a thin oak, she stared out across the rugged land. The view was spectacular. But she didn't want to enjoy it without her father.

"You be more careful."

Startled, she spun around, her fist pressed in between her breasts, cursing her stupidity. So engrossed in finding out where the tunnel went, she hadn't thought to bring a gun. Squatting on the rocks above her were Redhawk and Quanah.

She glanced around, the skin puckering between her brows. "How...how did you find me here?"

The Quahadi leader stared at her a moment then shrugged. "I Comanche."

A slow smile curled the corners of her mouth up. "You are speaking to me in English."

He nodded. They crawled from their perch and entered

the small grotto. The enclosed space was now even tighter with the two large Indians sitting inside.

"After we leave, Quanah ask to learn more words. He not understand all you say, and he no like."

She sat facing them, wondering why they'd returned, but was a little afraid to ask. These men were so intimidating. And she was alone.

"We find Reecardo," Redhawk said.

She nodded, her eyes filling with tears. "Thank you. I couldn't bear the thought of him out there. Or animals..."

"He buried with Comanche honor," Quanah said.

Her gaze went from one to the other. "What does that mean?"

"Comanche custom to—" He rolled himself into a ball, not knowing the words to explain.

"You folded him up?"

He nodded. "Yes, fold. Blankets tied around him. Three squaws take to final resting place. Horse and saddle buried too—so he reach hunting grounds."

Her lips trembled, and she pressed them together. What they had done for her father was indeed an honor. She blinked several times, ignoring the burning inside her nose from trying not to cry. "Did you come back to tell me?"

Quanah nodded. "I move Quahadis. No safe. You daughter of great man, and Black Wolf is Comanche brother. We honor his blood with you, Comanche daughter."

She frowned. "I don't understand. Who is Black Wolf?"

"Black Wolf is Comanche name for Reecardo."

He shook his head and glanced at Redhawk who nodded back. "Black Wolf like Quanah, not all Comanche. Quanah has white blood. Reecardo mixed blood too—Comanche and Mexican. Very honorable. Mexicans good friend to Quahadis. Black Wolf's mother was Comanche squaw. She die when he born. His father took Mexican squaw after, but she no good."

Her breath stuck in her throat. Her father had told her the same story.

"I still can't believe he's gone," she whispered, staring into the fire. Not even the warm heat filling the small cave took the cold from her body.

"White soldier kill Black Wolf?" Redhawk asked.

She nodded. "They attacked the house yesterday afternoon. After they...after killing my father. Dean was hurt, but it wasn't serious." She frowned, unable to move her gaze from the soft orange flames.

"They not gone," Quanah added. "Meet up with bad Indians. Young braves want to prove strength. No good."

"That's what I was afraid of." She sighed. "We can hold them off for a while, but our bullets are almost gone." She forced herself to meet his light gray gaze. "Thank you, again, for taking care of my father." She smoothed out her dress and gave him a sad smile. "And for the clothes. My dress is beautiful."

"You like Comanche squaw. We leave now. Not safe for Quahadis. Go to other home. Your cattle will be returned soon."

She smiled. "Thank you, Quanah. As long as I am here, you and your people will be welcome. If you are agreeable, I would also like to continue trading beef for skins and protection."

He nodded. "Is good to trade." He held out his hand to her. In his palm lay a thin-bladed knife.

She picked it up and turned it over. The blade was newly sharpened, and the handle was made from what looked like an antler. The six-inch length was perfect for her.

"I give you," Quanah said in a low voice, his tone pulling

her gaze to his. "You fight well. Strength of Black Wolf in blood. Comanche blood strong."

They rose without a sound. She raised her gaze from the small knife, but they were gone.

She glanced back down at the knife and tightly clasped the handle in her fist. The blade was a good one. Glancing outside, she realized how late it had gotten. With a soft sigh, she put out the fire then walked back to the tunnel. Just as she crouched to enter the dank, narrow space, she heard the scrape of a heeled boot against the rock opening behind her.

"I think you'll be comin' with me."

She slowly turned to see Sergeant Taylor squatting in the rocky opening with his pistol aimed at her.

PAUL WALKED through the front door, and Dean sat up, rubbing his eyes. Still bleary eyed, Dean glanced around the room and frowned. "Where's Anna?"

Paul's steps slowed then picked up pace as he strode toward the well room. The door was still wide open, but everything looked the same as when he'd left. He moved back into the large room and threw a couple of logs on the dying fire. "If she left the house, she didn't come to the barn." He turned and faced Dean. "Where would she go? She knows it isn't safe to leave."

"Took her father's death hard, maybe harder than we thought."

"Daniels!" Taylor's voice hollered from outside. "I have something here that belongs to you."

With dread, he made his way toward the window. With one finger, he peeked between the quilt and the windowsill. In the middle of the yard stood Taylor, trying to hold a struggling Anna against him with one arm, a gun in the other. Fury rose inside him, and he shoved one of his pistols into the sleeve of his coat. Without hesitating, he marched through the front door.

Holding his arms away from his body, he walked toward them, Anna's gaze widened as she shook of her head.

"What do you want, Taylor? The land? Cattle?" He dropped his arms to his sides and let the pistol slide down his coat sleeve, the end of the barrel resting in the center of his palm. "Let her go, and we will walk away. You can have it all."

His gaze met Taylor's above her head. Paul didn't like the wild gleam in his eyes. He recognized the same look in Taylor's father's eyes. The man standing before him was no longer a soldier, but a crazy man. Crazy from greed and the driving need to prove he was better than everyone. Better than him.

A quick glance at Hardin, and the gunslinger stepped back behind the line of Indians, dropping his head in a subtle nod.

What was he up to?

The Indians moved forward and spread out. From the corner of his eyes, he watched as two of them tried to move around him. Suddenly, they jerked and, like a felled tree, fell face down in the snow. Comanche arrows still quivered in their backs. He counted the remaining men, but the odds were still too high. He hoped it was Quanah or Redhawk shooting behind him—and that they wouldn't stop. Only one of him against Taylor, Hardin, and seven more renegades wasn't an encouraging thought.

Taylor's eyes widened, and he pulled Anna closer. Running the gun down her cheek, he whispered loud enough for Paul to hear. "And you, my dear. You, I will take as well. You will be mine to do with as I please. Ask your man there what I can do to a woman. I learned many things from my father, but torment was his specialty."

He stepped back, pulling her with him. He glanced at the

remaining Indians then back to Paul. "Now, I think I'll let my friends here take care of the both of you. A couple of them are Comanche. Their methods of torture are almost as bad as the Sioux. Maybe even the Apache." He backed them up a few more steps, and several more Indians took his place.

CHAPTER 18

Paul had gotten himself into a bad situation; there was no denying it. He allowed them to catch him out in the open with no cover and no hope of pulling down his gun without taking some lead. From behind him came the soft whisper of wood sliding over wood. He hoped it was Dean climbing out through a side window.

Two more braves went down with arrows in their faces and necks. From where he stood, he could see Taylor pulling Anna backward as she struggled against him, but he still couldn't see Hardin. Trying to find him, he stepped sideways.

"Don't move, Daniels, or I might change my mind and kill her instead of you! I can always find me another woman. Just keep your feet planted right there!"

Dean rushed from the side of the house, and Taylor, who took his eyes off Paul for only a second, turned and fired two shots at Dean. From the angle of Dean's fall, Paul saw the spreading blood stain across his chest and side.

"Dean!" Anna screamed and tried to lunge for him, but Taylor's grasp around her was too strong. She fought like a hellcat, scratching and clawing, as his other arm wrapped around her waist. "Let me go!"

Taylor seemed to be gaining control as he tightened his grip, trying to stop her frantic movements. The Indians went crazy, yelling and screaming as they charged Paul with knives.

Paul let his pistol drop firmly into the palm of his hand and fired at the two on his left. They went down, and two more sprang forward to take their place. He fired again, but that shot missed. His bullet cut through one's thigh and another clipped the shoulder.

Arrows rained through the sky, and three Indians fell to the ground, several arrows protruding from their upper bodies. Another ran forward then stopped as he glanced toward the house. His eyes widened and he turned, running into the trees.

Paul didn't want to hit Anna, but anger churned his insides when he saw Taylor's gun pressed against her temple. He remembered the boy he'd grown up with, thinking of him as his older brother. He recalled every hit and push. He had scars on his back and thighs from Taylor burning him with a poker. He could still hear Taylor's laughter while he writhed in agony on the floor.

He set his sights on the only part of Taylor he could see without hitting her. His finger pulled back on the trigger, but only slightly. Taylor's eyes widened, and he met Paul's narrowed gaze.

"You wouldn't dare. If she dies, it's on your hands." He took a step back, pulling her with him.

She glanced at Paul, her gaze steady. With a twist of one arm, she elbowed Taylor and jerked free, the force moving her out of Paul's way. When she fell away, all he saw was blood covering the back of her dress. When she stumbled, his heart stilled and ran toward her. Her hands brushed the ground as she regained her balance then continued running toward him. He held her tightly against him. Taylor stumbled forward a step but remained upright. His body hunched over, and his hands clasped around the small knife protruding from his stomach.

Taylor staggered forward again then fell on his knees with a frown. Looking up at Paul, Taylor blinked several times as if his vision was blurred. "This wasn't supposed to... happen." Taylor fell forward, hitting the ground with a soft *thud*.

Anna turned in Paul's embrace, wrapping her arms around his neck with a sob. Not one for comforting, he continued to hold her. He didn't want to let her go, and that frightened him. He buried his nose in her hair and breathed in. She smelled like fresh air and smoke, but with Hardin still out there, this wasn't yet finished.

With a quick glance around the yard, he realized all the renegades, as well as Taylor, were dead. His gaze landed on Dean who lay where he fell, unmoving.

As if reading his mind, she pulled away, her face dirty and streaked with tears. With a gasp, she whispered Dean's name and ran toward him. He followed.

Paul turned him over and examined the wound. The bleeding had slowed thanks to the snow, but the injury was serious enough. The bullet entered high on the right side of his chest, tearing through the muscles in his shoulder. Thankfully, the side wound was only a scrape.

Dean coughed several times then groaned, pushing a cold clump of snow off his forehead. "Got me good, didn't he, Lieutenant?"

Paul ignored the title and gave the kid a smile. "I've seen worse. Gonna have to dig out the bullet. Think you're up for it?"

Dean hesitated then gave him a quick nod. "I saw how you were with Redhawk. Trust you to fix me up."

Paul leaned closer and in a low whisper added, "We're not out of the woods yet. Don't know who was helping us by killin' the renegades, and Hardin's disappeared."

Anna dropped down into a squat. "That was Hardin? John Wesley Hardin—the gunslinger?"

Paul nodded. "He stepped out of my line of sight before the shootin' started. He was here for a reason, and I figure we'll soon find out what it was."

Dean coughed again then raised up on his left elbow and glanced around. "Who got Taylor?"

"Anna stabbed him with a knife."

Dean's eyes widened. "You need to start adding notches to that gun of yours."

She smiled, but her face was a bit green. "That's a stupid, immature thing to do. Besides, I didn't have a gun. I had a knife."

Paul stared down at her. She was sure one to ride the trail with.

Movement by the porch caught Paul's attention, and he started to raise his pistol but stopped when he saw Quanah and Redhawk standing in front of the porch with arrows drawn, staring at something behind them.

"Anna, move behind me," he whispered.

Without questioning why, she scooted around him and pressed her hand against the bloody wound on Dean's shoulder. Paul gripped the gun's handle and swung around into a fighting stance, holding his gun near his hip. Standing just inside the clearing was John Hardin. He took another step.

"Stop there, Hardin. Seems to me you've attached yourself to the wrong sort of people."

Hardin's mustache rose as he smiled. It wasn't a pleasant

smile. He held out his hands, but they were empty, his guns still holstered across his chest. "Not here to do anyone harm."

Anna peered out from behind Paul's legs. "Coming from you, I find that hard to believe, Mr. Hardin."

"Spirited woman you got there, Daniels. Hope you can handle her," Hardin said.

"What do you want?"

The gunslinger took another step toward them but was stopped by the twang of an arrow as it flew into the ground in front of his feet. He gave the Indians a quick glance, then turned his dark gaze back on Paul. "Heard what Taylor was planning and thought I'd tag along. Didn't cotton to him much…and for me, that's saying something. Believe it or not, I only wanted to meet you."

Anna glanced up at Paul, but he kept his eyes on Hardin. The man was too fast with a gun for him to look away even for a second. She rose and stepped up beside him.

"Why would you want to meet me?" Paul asked, not trusting the man in front of him one bit.

Hardin let his arms fall to his sides. "Served on the side of the Union during the war. Met Wild Bill Hickok during the Battle of Pea Ridge when my unit came under heavy fire. Hickok saved the lot of us. Owe him my life. He was up on the ridge, taking out one Reb after another. I was there when you shot the soldier crawling up the far side of the ridge. Your shot was every bit as good as Hickok's—and saved his life. All I want is to shake your hand, then I'll leave."

Paul remembered taking that shot, but he hadn't realized Hickok was the sharpshooter up on the ridge. The man standing before them wasn't anything like the cold-blooded killer he'd heard of. This man, although still dangerous, was almost likable. Maybe if he got to know him he'd think differently…but for now, a hand shake was better than a bullet.

He hesitated then slid his gun down into his holster and stepped forward. The Comanches behind them still had their arrows drawn, and he trusted them to have his back if needed. And to protect Anna. He recognized the weapon she used to kill Taylor. Only one of them could have given the scalping knife to her. He extended his hand toward Hardin who took it in a firm grasp and shook it once.

"You're a good man, Daniels, with a good thing here. If you should ever need help, I'll be there."

Hardin glanced once more at the warriors standing behind them. With precise movements, he walked backward toward the trees, turned, and disappeared.

"My behind is numb, and my shoulder is aching something awful. Can we go inside the house now?" Dean grumbled.

Paul glanced over at Dean who had lain back on the ground. Redhawk and Quanah were also gone, leaving as silently as they arrived.

Together, Paul and Anna picked Dean up and with his arms draped around their shoulders, carried him into the house. As before, she gathered the supplies and boiled the water while Paul sewed him up.

While Dean slept, Anna warmed up the tortillas and biscuits from the night before. While they were eating, the bawling of cows sounded nearby. Paul shoved the last biscuit into his mouth, shoved his arms into his coat, and grabbed the rifle leaning in the corner. Without a backward glance, he left.

Pulling on her buffalo robe, she hurried outside after him to find cows everywhere. Near the barn, Paul stood talking to two Indians. With a few shrugs and arm swings, Paul nodded and made his way through the swarm of brown bodies.

He stopped at the bottom of the porch stairs. "Your cattle.

They only had about three-quarters of the herd by the time Quanah found them, so they're returning what's left."

She stared at the milling cattle. "What are we going to do with them? They won't fit anywhere. "

"I'm going to take them to Camp Wichita."

"Not by yourself you're not."

He smiled. "No, not by myself. Quanah made sure his men would help, and I promised to speak with the colonel on their behalf."

She nodded and smiled. "That's a good idea. Quanah and Redhawk have helped me more than I will ever be able to repay." She glanced up at the darkening sky. "You'll leave tomorrow morning, surely?"

"We will leave before dawn."

She watched him walk back to where the Indians had gathered near the barn. There were ten men, eleven with Paul. As she watched him, for some unexplained reason she had a bad feeling she'd never see him again.

With a sigh, she went back inside to check on Dean.

Paul pushed the gate closed behind the last cow at Camp Wichita. The weather had cooperated during the short drive, with the temperature rising to above freezing.

"Daniels!"

He turned to see Colonel Davidson walking toward him with a smile. "Damned good timing, son! We just butchered our last steer two days ago and wondered if I was goin' to have to go hunting!"

"That'd be some hunt to find enough meat to feed everyone here, Colonel."

Davidson clapped him on the back and led him toward the headquarters building. "Come on in and I'll get you Flores's money."

"Sir, Flores was killed a couple of days ago."

"Damn. What happened?"

Paul accepted the cup of coffee from the private who poured another and handed it to Davidson. "You missing a sergeant and a couple of privates?"

"Hell, yes I am! Where are they?"

"Dead."

"What in God's name happened out there, Daniels?" Davidson leaned against the front edge of his desk.

"It's a long story, sir. Sergeant Taylor's the man behind the raids at Flores's place. He wanted the ranch and figured the easiest way to get it was to take away the cattle and horses."

"He kill Flores too?"

Paul shook his head. "Wade Phillips' brother killed him. Reckon' he's high-tailed it back to Texas by now."

"Comanches aren't goin' to like any of this." He scrubbed his face. "Flores was keepin' them calm."

"I don't think you'll be havin' much problem with Quanah. Anna is Ricardo's daughter, and part Comanche herself. Don't know if she's planning on stayin' or returning to her stepfather's Rancho in Texas, but while she's here, they'll behave. She's one helluva gal, sir."

Davidson gave him a crooked grin. "Sounds like there's somethin' between the two of you."

Paul shook his head. "Just admirin' is all."

The colonel reached behind him and grabbed an envelope, handing it to Paul. "Can't thank you enough, son, for what you've done. Sorry to hear about Flores. I'll miss our talks. I do, however, think there's a young lady waitin' for you back at that ranch."

Paul left headquarters, stuffing the envelope full of Anna's money into his inner coat pocket, as he walked to the stables. He outfitted his horse but didn't mount. Instead, he stared at the stall wall facing him.

He'd taken his time driving the cattle here, but the only thing on his mind had been Anna. He kept trying to convince himself that a relationship with her would never work. Thanks to Taylor, he now knew his mother had never chosen to be with the man he'd grown up thinking his father.

If he were honest with himself, he'd admit to himself that the only reason he'd chosen to take the cattle and leave for good was because he was scared. He never thought he had what it took to be a husband, and the idea of being a father had terrified him.

With Anna by his side, he knew he could be both...and so much more. She made him believe in himself, and he wanted to spend the rest of his life showing her how much he loved her.

"ANNA, if you keep pacing, you're going to wear a very large hole in the floor," Dean grumbled.

"Why hasn't he come back, Dean?" Anna stopped for only a moment then continued pacing in front of the fireplace. "He should've been back yesterday. The Comanches who helped him arrived last night. Why didn't he?"

Dean sighed. "For the hundredth time, I don't know. Paul's a drifter, a wanderer. It's in his blood, and no one can change that."

She fell onto the sofa, her shoulders slumped forward as she stared into the crackling fire. "He didn't even say goodbye..."

The day after Paul left, she realized just how much he'd become a part of her life. She didn't want to go back to Texas. Her place was here, taking care of her father's ranch. She wanted to learn about her heritage, and get to know the only family she had left—the Comanches.

But none of it would mean anything if Paul wasn't beside her. She loved him.

"Anna," Dean said.

"Hmm?" She continued to stare into the flames.

"Anna, you need to see this."

With indifference, she rose and walked to the window where Dean, holding one side of the quilt covering the opening, was smiling at something outside. She moved to the other side and pulled the quilt away. In the center of the yard stood a man and his horse.

With a quiet sob, she jerked open the door and ran outside, stopping at the edge of the top porch stair. "Paul?"

With a graceful motion, he swung his leg behind him and climbed down. He dropped the reins and walked toward her.

She met him halfway, her nerves a jumbled mess. She shivered in the evening chill as he stepped up to her.

"I'm sorry, Anna." He pulled an envelope from inside his coat and held it out.

She frowned, glancing at the yellowed paper and, with a shaking hand, took it from him. "You returned to give me an envelope?"

"It's the money for the herd."

"I know what it is."

"I was going to have a soldier bring it to you..."

She took another step forward, close enough to touch him. "But?"

"I couldn't do it." He closed his eyes a moment then shoved his hat high on his forehead. "I couldn't leave you, Anna Sanchez."

"Flores. And you couldn't leave me why?"

Pulling her to him, he wrapped his arms around her shoulders and stared down at her. He raised his hand and let his fingers run through her long black hair, the strands as soft as he dreamed they would be. "I've wanted to do this since the day we met."

She smiled up at him, her brown eyes sparkling. "Now I'm going to do something I've wanted to do since the other morning." She stood on her tiptoes. Wrapping her arms around his neck, she kissed him.

He lifted her up, wrapping her securely against him, and deepened the kiss. He finally found what he'd spent his entire life searching for. Love.

Setting her down before him, he held her face between his hands, his thumbs caressing her cold cheeks. "I love you, Anna Flores. I've never said those words to another human being before, but I do. I love you."

She bit her bottom lip and smiled. "I love that you're strange. It will keep our marriage interesting."

He chuckled. "I don't recall proposing marriage—"

She lightly slapped his chest. "Oh shush. You know we're getting married." Her mock scowl disappeared in a wide smile. "I love you too. I want to be the person to make up for all the bad things you've had to suffer."

He feathered another kiss over her lips then nibbled on her ear. "Even if there are people in my past who want to hurt me? Taylor's father won't rest until he has revenge for his son's death. I have nothing to give you but myself. Anna, my mother was Indian. There are those who wouldn't understand, who would lash out at us or worse."

She sighed. "All I want is you, Paul. What little I have is yours, including my heart." She brushed his cheek with the back of one hand. "You aren't the only one with Indian blood. I'm proud of who I am, and I don't care what other people think." She frowned up at him with a crooked smile. "Does that mean our children will be full-blooded?"

"I don't think it works that way, but I like the thought of

children." He glanced over at Dean who was walking very slowly onto the porch. "Speaking of children..."

She turned her head and smiled as Dean grumbled, frustrated and irritable from having stayed inside for three days. "He's doing well. No infection."

"Have you thought about whether you want to return to Texas or stay here?" Paul whispered in her ear.

She smiled up at him, her cheeks pink and flushed. She was so beautiful. "I'll go wherever you are."

He wrapped his arm around her shoulders and turned her toward the house. "Then I guess we're already home."

I hope you enjoyed *Trail of Secrets.* Turn the page to read the excerpt from the next book in the series, *Mia's Misfits,* or use the link to buy it.
http://tiny.cc/wt-abc-misfits

I need your help.
Reviews help readers find books, so please use the link below to leave a review on Amazon but
BookBub and GoodReads are also great options.
http://www.amazon.com/review/create-review?&asin=B019DCY7CM

MIA'S MISFITS

EXCERPT

Chapter 1

New York City, New York, 1880

Mia Bradley finished writing the last sentence of her history lesson on the large chalkboard at the front of her classroom. She laid the short chalk stub on top of the others in the small tray on the wall then wiped the white dust from her fingers on the damp rag hanging from the hook beneath the chalk tray. She turned to face her students.

Hearing the other classroom doors open and the older students begin their trek toward the dining room, she glanced up at the clock. She turned to her five small charges and walked around to the front of her desk. "All right, my dears. Before you leave to go to supper, I want you to tell me what I've written on the board." She glanced at each of the children's faces as they stared at the block letters behind her. "Can anyone tell me what it says?"

One little girl hesitantly raised her arm, and Mia bit back her smile. Of all the children, she hadn't expected Amanda to volunteer. Normally, the shy blonde-haired five-year-old stayed silent while the others answered her questions.

"Amanda? Can you tell me what I've written on the chalkboard?"

"Am-America's fight for indi-indi-pen-independence," she stuttered in her soft voice.

Mia gave her a wide smile. "Very good, Amanda! That's perfect! Tomorrow, we will learn about how America fought a terrible war against England to become the great country we are today. Now, put your primers in your cubicles by the door and you are all dismissed for supper."

"Thank you, Miss Bradley," the class said in unison. At once, five sets of feet scurried and scuffed across the scarred wooden floor as they raced to the door. Chuckling to herself, she walked around her desk again, plucked the rag from the hook and wiped the chalkboard clean. Rubbing away the cramping pain in her right arm, which usually appeared with any repetitive work, she organized her lessons for the next day. With a quick glance around the room, she turned the light switch and closed the door behind her.

Not hungry, she returned to the room she shared with Katriona, who taught life skills to the other students, as well as Jessamine and Leanna, two other teachers at the orphanage. She lay down on her bed. The news Madam Wigg had given them earlier that afternoon had been beyond unsettling. How could someone as vibrant and full of life as Wiggie be dying?

Mia pressed her face into her pillow and sobbed, letting loose the tears that had threatened to make an appearance all afternoon. Wiggie was the only mother she had ever known. Nothing ever seemed to stand in the woman's way. She had never seen her sick a day in her life. How could she be dying? And for her to suggest they should leave to find new schools to teach in? It was preposterous!

Mia lay on the bed, exhausted from crying, exhausted from feeling. From what seemed like far away, she heard footsteps and the opening and closing of doors as she made a vow to herself. She refused to accept Wiggie was dying and would stay and make sure Wiggie had everything she needed for a full recovery. She couldn't leave to become a mail-order bride just to find a new position, knowing that Wiggie faced a death sentence, although deep down, Mia couldn't help but wonder if this was simply a ploy to get them to move on with their own lives. Her last thought before she drifted off was that quite possibly Wiggie wanted 'her girls' to find out there was something more to life than just teaching...like love? Mia wrapped the blanket around her tighter with a tiny smile playing over her lips. Of course, she would. That's exactly what Wiggie would want.

A constant pounding intruded and Mia jerked in her sleep, the recurring nightmare refusing to release its hold on her. She lay curled up on the floor of a large, unfamiliar room. Someone close by yelled, hollering nonsense words, but she knew the pain was about to begin and braced herself. One, two, three—there it was. The first stabbing kick, then another. The agony breathtaking.

The pounding returned, this time louder and more insistent. Voices intruded. Familiar voices. She felt as if she were trying to breathe under water. She thrashed out with her arms and legs, fighting for air, fighting against something she couldn't even name.

"Mia!" her roommate, Katriona's, voice hissed in the darkness as she shook her.

Mia shoved her friend's hand away from her shoulder. "I'm awake. I'm awake." She grabbed Kat's hand, her eyes wide. "Is it Xenia? Has she come back?"

"No. As far as I know, she's still missing."

Mia pulled her hand away, wearily rubbing her eyes. "I was sure she'd have returned by now."

"We all were, and I thought you'd never wake up. Poor Brian has been knocking on the door for almost ten minutes."

Mia sat up and swung her legs to the floor, automatically reaching for her night rail. "And why didn't you answer it sooner?" she asked, shoving first one arm then her other into the sleeves. She tied the silk sash around her waist and slipped her feet into her slippers.

"Because I was trying to sleep, too. I couldn't take the knocking any longer, so I answered the door."

Mia ignored her friend's flippant remark and tried to finger brush her hair into some order. "It must be serious for the children to have been awakened." She opened the door to see Brian standing there wringing his hands, his cute freckled face scrunched tight in worry. Even his normally slicked back coiffure stood on end, a telling sign to the poor child's agitation.

She dropped to her knees in front of him and opened her arms wide while Katriona hurried past them and down the hall. With a stifled whimper, he stepped into Mia's embrace, his small body shaking like a leaf in a high gale. She rubbed his back and rested her cheek against his soft curls.

"Whatever's happened, I'm sure will work out just fine. You'll see. Miss Katriona, Madam Wigg, and I will make it all right in no time." She gently pushed him away, held him by the shoulders and gave him a smile as Katriona hurried back toward them. "Let me talk a moment with Miss Katriona and then we will go."

He nodded but didn't say anything, only bit his lower lip and continued wringing his hands.

Mia turned around and frowned at Katriona, noticing for

the first time that her short blonde hair was in a bit more disarray than usual. "What has happened?"

The preacher and the orphan. Nothing in common but pain, loneliness, and hope. Will that be enough? To read more about Mia and Josiah, click or go to the link below.

http://tiny.cc/wt-abc-misfits

If you love historical romances, sign up for my reader list, and as a thank you, I'll send you the prequel, a novella, in my Western Trails series.

To download, go to http://tiny.cc/nl-histwest

LUCIE: BRIDE OF TENNESSEE

PREQUEL, MAIL-ORDER BRIDES OF THE SOUTHWEST

http://tiny.cc/mobsw-amob-lucie

To provide for herself and her younger brother, Lucie Croft accepts a mail-order bride contract in Chattanooga. Fate has other things in store for her when her intended groom dies before her arrival. Desperate and homeless, Lucie relies on the kindness of a local hotel owner, Sebastian McCord. Overwhelmed as a single father and intrigued by Lucie, Sebastian agrees to marry her. Will the couple create a loving family or does fate have yet another turn in the road?

This book is also #16 in the American Mail-Order Brides series.

HEART OF THE SOLDIER

WWII ROMANCE WITH MAGICAL REALISM

http://tiny.cc/heart-soldier

American Resistance fighter, Caroline Grayson, can "see" the war against the Nazis in her mind. After discovering an American soldier behind enemy lines, she must choose between one lone soldier or the lives of those trying to escape the tortures of the Nazi death camps.

Called to defend his country, Stuart Williams finds himself on the front line against the Nazi war machine. When an intriguing Resistance fighter puts her life in danger to help him, he must decide if his first allegiance is to the army or to the beauty who came to his aid.

Will Caroline's magic bring them together or will Nazi brutality sever them forever?

ALSO BY HEIDI VANLANDINGHAM

IN READING ORDER

For all Buy Links: www.heidivanlandingham.com

Western Trails series

Trail of Hope

Trail of Courage

Trail of Secrets

Mia's Misfits

Mia's Misfits is also in ABC Mail-Order Bride series

Trail of Redemption

American Mail-Order Bride series &

Prequel to Mail-Order Brides of the Southwest

Lucie: Bride of Tennessee

Mail-Order Brides of the Southwest series

The Gambler's Mail-Order Bride

The Bookseller's Mail-Order Bride

The Marshal's Mail-Order Bride

The Woodworker's Mail-Order Bride

The Gunslinger's Mail-Order Bride

The Agent's Mail-Order Bride

WWII

Heart of the Soldier

Flight of the Night Witches

Natalya

Aleksandra

Book 3 available in Fall 2020

Raisa

Of Mystics and Mayhem series

In Mage We Trust

Saved By the Spell

The Curse That Binds

Mistletoe Kisses

Music and Moonlight

Sleighbells and Snowflakes

Angels and Ivy

Nutcrackers and Sugarplums

Box Sets Available

Mail-Order Brides of the Southwest: 3-Book collection

Mistletoe Kisses: 4-book collection

Western Trails: 2-book collection

ABOUT THE AUTHOR

Author Heidi Vanlandingham writes sweet, action-packed stories that take place in the Wild West, war-torn Europe, and otherworldly magical realms. Her love of history finds its way into each book, and her characters are lovable, strong, and diverse.

Growing up in Oklahoma and living one year in Belgium gave Heidi a unique perspective regarding different cultures. She still lives in Oklahoma with her husband and youngest son. Her favorite things in life are laughter, paranormal romance books, music, and long road trips.

Heidi currently writes multiple genres but mostly fixates on fantasy/paranormal and historical romance.

For more about Heidi: www.heidivanlandingham.com

- amazon.com/Heidi-Vanlandingham/e/B00BI5NPA8?tag=heidivanlaaut-20
- bookbub.com/authors/heidi-vanlandingham
- goodreads.com/heidivanlandingham
- facebook.com/heidi.vanlandingham.author
- instagram.com/heidivanlandingham_author
- pinterest.com/Hvanlandingham

Made in United States
Orlando, FL
06 March 2022

15434435R00117